JUDGMENT

JUDGMENT
THE

Feather and Bone

The Crow Chronicles

Clem Martini

KCP FICTION
An Imprint of Kids Can Press

KCP Fiction is an imprint of Kids Can Press

Kids Can Press acknowledges the financial support of the Government of Ontario, through the Ontario Media Development Corporation's Ontario Book Initiative; the Ontario Arts Council; the Canada Council for the Arts; and the Government of Canada, through the BPIDP, for our publishing activity.

Published in Canada by	Published in the U.S. by
Kids Can Press Ltd.	Kids Can Press Ltd.
29 Birch Avenue	2250 Military Road
Toronto, ON M4V 1E2	Tonawanda, NY 14150

www.kidscanpress.com

Edited by Charis Wahl
Designed by Marie Bartholomew
Printed and bound in Canada

CM 06 0 9 8 7 6 5 4 3 2 1
CM PA 07 0 9 8 7 6 5 4 3 2 1

Library and Archives Canada Cataloguing in Publication

Martini, Clem, 1956–
            The judgment / Clem Martini.

(Feather and bone)

ISBN 978-1-55337-756-6 (bound).   ISBN 978-1-55337-757-3 (pbk.)

1. Crows—Juvenile fiction. I. Title. II. Series: Martini, Clem, 1956–
Feather and bone.

PS8576.A7938J83 2006   jC813'.54   C2005-907022-6

Kids Can Press is a *l☺rus*™ Entertainment company

To Cheryl, Chandra and Miranda, many thanks
and much love.

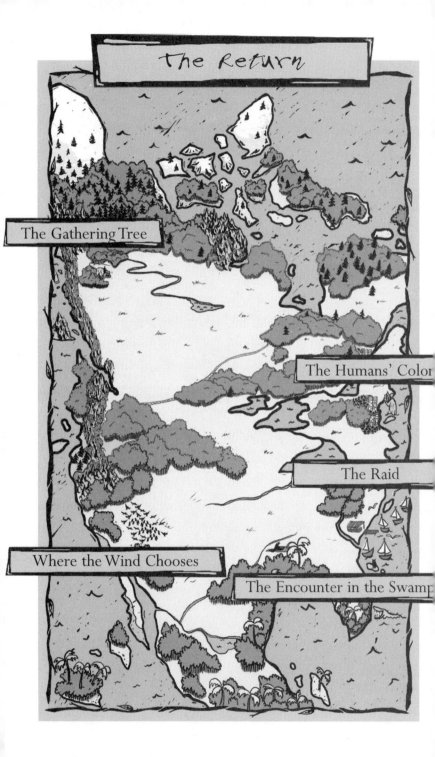

The Return

The Gathering Tree

The Humans' Colony

The Raid

Where the Wind Chooses

The Encounter in the Swamp

Part One

chapter *1*

Listen.

It's twilight, as only twilight was in First Times, a long, hushed, magical stretch. A halted breath between day and night. First Time Owl glides through a forest dark as death and silent as the delicate descent of falling snow. It is the beginning of the long evening hunt.

There is little that First Time Owl's probing orange eyes miss as he scans the thick mat of bram- bles and branches. Something dark darts between two towering spruce, and with barely a twitch of his gray-and-black striped feathers, Owl changes course and slides between the trees.

The dark shape separates from the trees and

takes the form of Great Crow. Within his beak he carries a bundle of twigs. In his talons, he clutches a wad of grass and bulrush down. Owl continues following at a distance, undetected, until at last he sees Great Crow stop to deposit the twigs, grass and down into a sheltered hollow in the crook of a balsam poplar. As Great Crow arranges the twigs, Owl retreats, quiet as mist rising from the river at dawn. Chuckling softly to himself, he thinks, "Oh ho, I needn't come back here tonight. Now that I know where Great Crow's nest is being built, I can return later for a longer, larger, much more satisfying meal. First the eggs. Then the mate. And finally Great Crow himself."

But just as there is no real beginning to a story — only the continuation of an earlier tale — nor any real end — just the brief pause for breath before the next account begins — know this: while Owl is watching Great Crow, he is part of a longer, more complicated story. He himself is being watched.

Who is watching? Great Crow's mate, Kaynu, and as First Time Owl flies off, thinking his private, hungry, owl thoughts, she leaps from the pine where she has hidden herself and flies directly to where Great Crow arranges the twigs. Quickly she informs him of what she saw. "Shouldn't we," she asks, "abandon our nest?"

"Abandon it?" Great Crow muses as he tucks a twig firmly into place. "No, but maybe it would be useful to build another."

With that, Great Crow and Kaynu fly deeper into the woods, to where light and warmth penetrate the twine of leaves and branches only rarely. There, above the confusion of coiling vines and creeping mosses, they commence assembling another, even bigger nest in a teetering, towering, thick-trunked fir.

Not to be deterred, Owl follows this activity as well. He sees the new nest and understands that Great Crow and Kaynu may have chosen to relocate. He congratulates himself on his watchfulness and says, "Patience is the father of every good meal. I will bide my time. When their nest is well and truly chosen, and their brood laid, then I will satisfy my hunger."

Are these the only participants in this story, then? No. The woods are dense and stretch in all directions. Animals roost throughout that twist and tangle, some in the trees, some in the rushes and some in the deep, dark cavities and cracks in the earth. Down among the bushes, near the thrusting roots of trees, paces restless, hungry Pine Marten. Able to scale tree trunks like a squirrel, able to skip a branch as nimbly as a chipmunk, he is always, always hungry, and he too eyes this second nest. His pink tongue traces the tips of his furry lips as he recollects that there is nothing he enjoys better than dining on egg. Like Owl, he bides his time and decides to return when the nest is built.

So, each day First Time Owl quietly loops back to check on the first and second nests. Each day he watches both growing steadily until, at long last, one spring day Great Crow appears to decide. Kaynu, heavy with eggs, heaves her immense body in among the carefully arranged twigs of the second nest and settles. Great Crow darts back and forth between the nest and the forest floor, carrying good eating of all kinds, and Owl nods his massive round head and snaps his beak shut. "This one," he chants to himself. "This one. This one is the very one."

So that night, late, in the dimness of the dark six, Owl returns, quiet as fear, quiet as grief, quiet as unspoken dread. He circles the second nest and finds no one. "All the better," he concludes. "Raid the nest first, savor the freshly laid eggs, then take the occupant when she returns."

He drops to the outer edge of the nest and peers down. Within that sacred circle he finds branches and brambles, feathers and mouse bones, fibers from the milkweed, fur from the rabbit's breast, thread from the spider's web — but not the slightest trace nor taste of egg. Irritated, he crouches closer, and discovers something he hadn't expected but that often arrives unexpectedly — his own death.

Pine Marten, so lithe and silent and supple among trees, had perched still as stone on an overhanging branch, awaiting the return of Great Crow and Kaynu. Sensing activity, he hadn't bothered looking, but instead pounced jaws agape upon that broad unprotected back of First Time Owl.

As he scampered away into the night, feathers fluttering from his toothy mouth, he reflected that Owl meat is perhaps not so sweet as Crow — but then again there's so much more of it.

And what of Great Crow and Kaynu? What of the eggs and the hatchlings and yearlings to come? Owl and Marten, so intent on the development of the large nests they saw growing in the tops of the trees, never thought to look for the third and smaller nest they hadn't detected in the dense brush of the tangled lower reaches.

Flight is only one of many ways to escape an enemy, my Cousins. Great Crow and all his descendants would never have lived and thrived if wit and will hadn't also played their part.

Let that sacred story guide us as we invoke this account of our latest desperate events, for there are many parallels. Flight through darkness, the use of one's wits, unlooked-for fortune and equally unlooked-for death.

Draw closer, Cousins. Draw closer and listen well. When we tell others of these past events, when we inform our chicks, when we gather at night with our Clan around us to remember, we should recollect everything.

So remember with me how this journey began. Remember our flight from the Plague. How sickness trickled and twisted into our life, as sap seeps from trees. How it clung to us as sap clings. How it issued after us, caught us and killed us.

Remember, Cousins, how our flocks were scattered by the sickness. How we flew without plan or preparation. How fate blew us from one roost to the next. How a new Clan and a new journey formed as we searched for this one that was lost: Kym ru Kemna ru Kinaar, captured by the human.

Remember, then, the discovery of Kym and the other unfortunates held captive in the deep, enclosed confines of the human roost. Remember the journey into the roost through tunnel and stealth. The escape out of the human's roost with fire and death.

Remember how in searching for one, we returned with many.

Retain every wing stroke of this long journey, each feather, each quill, the fortunes and misfortunes that eventually led us to this particular fork on this particular branch of the story.

Perched among the trees at the center of the sprawling, massive human colony. Having escaped from the fire and the fear of the collapsing human roost. Scouts from the Collection — Kuper's immense flock of Crow fanatics — sent to find us, captured. Kyp injured. All of us wondering how to proceed, and where.

Kyp ru Kurea ru Kinaar, his already lean body made leaner still by his recovery from the fire, perched, thinking. His feathers singed, his lungs seared, his throat scarred.

I studied him as he clung to the branch that day, seeming especially frail. A hard gust rattled the tree, and he teetered briefly to his left side, the side of his shorter leg. He gripped the perch more tightly as he addressed us.

"Before we fly," he rasped at last, "we must come to a decision. These two" — he nodded at the two scouts — "sent by the Collection to find us and report back. What should we do with them?" He glanced around.

"What should we do?" Erkala repeated grimly, looking up from her preening. "Kill them, of course," she pronounced in her curious, clipped accent and whetted her beak against a branch.

Thinking back, I probably agreed with her. It wasn't something I would welcome. It would be bad luck to start our flight from the human's colony in this manner — but what other solution was there? Kaf sniffed his disapproval but said nothing. Kym looked as though she might have wished to speak but didn't feel she had earned the right yet, having just joined the flock.

Kyp shook his head. "No. I don't want to do that."

Erkala's glance took in the rest of the council. "They can't be allowed to return to the Collection."

Kyf traced a faint line in the perch with one claw and shrugged reluctantly. "I agree with Erkala. What other choice have we?"

Kyp cleared his throat. "So far, the Collection hasn't caught a single one of us," he argued. "If we kill these ones now, when we don't have to ..." He stopped and shook his head. "How do we explain that to ourselves later?"

Kyf snorted. "That big one. That Chooser one for the Collection. Kuper, who calls himself Urku. Don't tell me he didn't *try* to kill you."

"But he was unsuccessful," Kyp pointed out, "and now what we have to resolve isn't what Kuper did or didn't do, but how we will act." Nobody seemed to have anything further to add, so Kyp flew to the branch where the scouts perched.

"Listen to me," Kyp began before halting again, wracked by painful coughs. He paused to swallow, then recommenced. "The council says kill you. My feeling is we haven't come to that. Tell your

Chooser, Kuper, we're leaving here. Tell him he has no reason to concern himself with us. We reject his invitation now, as we did before. We have no interest in joining him. We're finished what we set out to do, and he won't see us again in this territory. We're returning home, many flights out of his range. Tell him we'll be far away by tomorrow. Do you understand?"

The two Crows nodded, too frightened to reply.

"If we see you again, spying on us. If you fly after us, if you trouble us in any way, and we catch you, I won't stop these others. You understand me?"

Erkala stared intently at Kyp as he spoke, then hopped forward on her perch. "You can't just let them go," she warned, her voice even.

Kyp met Erkala's gaze, and an unspoken struggle between these two continued through the silence. Suddenly Kyp turned and leaped upon the strangers, his neck outstretched and his beak gaping. The two scouts shrieked and squirmed, but surrounded by us, they didn't dare put up any fight. In a flash he had plucked feathers from their tails and wings. The two hollered with alarm and pain, and then, as Kyp returned to his perch, looked to see if the rest of us were going to attack as well.

"Now go!" Kyp commanded after dropping the feathers from his beak. "I'll be setting these younger ones after you in a few moments, to make sure you haven't lingered. If they catch you, they can do with you as they like."

The strangers examined their damaged wings.

"Go!" Kyp shouted, even louder, his voice raw.

The scouts leaped from the branch but, after executing a few frantic, ineffectual strokes, lurched only as far as the next tree. It was clear their ability to steer or direct flight had been ruined by Kyp's attack and would remain impaired until their next molt.

I watched as they continued their pathetic zig-zagging journey from one tree to the next and nodded to myself. "It'll take them forever to get back to Kuper like that."

"*If* they get back," Kyf added. "Any hawk that catches sight of those two will eat well."

Erkala studied their departure a few moments, then abruptly turned, dropped from the branch and flew away.

An uncomfortable silence followed as we watched her leave. Kaf turned back to Kyp and shrugged. "Still. It's likely that they'll eventually reach Kuper. When they do, the Collection will come."

"Of course, they'll come after us," Kyp whispered, trying to save what little voice remained. "Kuper knows where we came from. He'll expect us to fly back that way."

"Which," I continued, after thinking a moment, "is why we'll be heading south instead."

"That's right," Kyp agreed quietly and turned to Kyf. "Gather everyone. Put out the call to those still foraging. We'll fly from here within the next sixth. At least that much of what I told those scouts was truth. I want to be as far from here as possible by the time those two get anywhere near Kuper."

chapter 2

Gathering wasn't the chore it might have been. Everyone had been preparing for days. Most of those foraging had remained close to the roost. We took count, asked for a blessing and in short time were high above the trees, winging south over the sprawling human colony.

Clouds lowered and snow began falling as we reached the southernmost edge of the colony. "So," I thought, "we arrived among humans in snow, and that's how we'll be leaving them as well."

For all the cold of the wind and the suddenness of our departure, there was very little grumbling from the flock. After our time spent among humans, and after the energy and efforts exerted freeing the captured Crows, there was almost a giddiness in our flight. It was as though all of us had been freed from long confinement.

And in a way we had. There are confinements of the body and there are confinements of the spirit. When you live too long among humans, you find yourself bound to human ways: rising when they rise, sleeping when they sleep, eating when and what they eat. It heightens your awareness of the human, but it deadens every other sense.

In any case, there is a sickness that comes from staying in one place too long, and only flight holds the cure. We flew and were happy. We called to one another and joked as we passed familiar landmarks of the human colony — landmarks we hoped never to see again. We followed the coastline south. As the salt air blew up off the water, I realized that I wouldn't be sorry to leave the smoke, soot and smell of humans behind.

Of course, the kind of joy we experienced lasts only a brief time. The human colonies and roosts are warmer than their surroundings. As we came to their fringes, it wasn't long before I saw and felt snow quite another way. It gathered on the tips of my wings, hampering flight and making me miserable. My shoulders ached. My belly grumbled. The snow had nothing to do with my belly grumbling — but still, it grumbled.

I glanced back at the flock. It was spread across the sky in disorganized, straggling lumps and clumps, and I reflected that we were not without our problems. At last Kyp signaled for us to stop, and we dropped toward a smallish grove of pine and fir.

As we settled on our various perches and waited for everyone to arrive, Kyf flew alongside me. "What do you think that one's doing there?" she inquired, nodding to a tree near the shore.

I glanced over. There — atop a sickly, wind-blasted beech tree — I saw one small, skinny-looking Crow perched all on his own.

I squinted but didn't recognize him. "Who is it?"

"One of the new ones," Kyf replied. "Kryk, I think his name is." She had, of course, picked up all the new ones' names almost as soon as they had joined us. I was still struggling.

"Yes, that's right," I said, making him out finally.

Kyp glanced up from his preening to observe the Crow we were talking about. "He's not roosting there, is he?"

We all stared out at the tree. The slight Crow seemed to have made himself comfortable, or as comfortable as you could be out on the windy end of an exposed branch. "I believe he *is*," Kyf murmured after a moment.

Kyp turned to Kaf. "Do me a favor. Swing by and tell that one if he won't shift to another tree to at least move in on the trunk. An owl glides by, it won't even have to slow down, it'll just swallow him and keep on going."

Kaf nodded and flew on over to relay the message.

Kyf watched her brother fly to the tree. The smaller Crow apparently listened, then shifted closer to the trunk, and we heard his voice call "Sorry!" to us as Kaf looped back.

"He's a character, that one," she remarked in a confidential tone.

"Who?" I asked, "Kryk?"

She nodded. "When we were resting earlier, he decided to help himself to a little rabbit."

Kyrt had just joined us, perched one branch up from me. "A rabbit?" he asked, puzzled. "You mean scavenge, right?"

"Well, if it was scavenge, it was a surprise to the rabbit. This one, this Kryk, landed on top of a big, heavy doe and set his talons into her. The rabbit gave a surprised shimmy, like she'd been bit by a midge, then took off *so fast* you would have thought she had just been eating shooting stars and pooping lightning. Brother Kryk isn't your burliest individual, but he's stubborn. He clung to the rabbit's rump, too frightened to let go, too proud to call for help, until at last the rabbit gave a frustrated hop and kick and off your Crow went, spinning head over talons into the bushes." Kyf turned to me. "You think that approach works where he comes from?"

"It can. If you're a little heavier, faster — and an *eagle*."

We enjoyed our laugh, but I saw Kyp watching carefully where Kaf left this Kryk, and I could see concern behind his laughter as he wondered just what kind of individual quirks he had inherited with this newly adopted group. Kym arrived at that point and dropped to a branch near Kyp.

"Good eating," Kyp greeted her, then asked, "Has anyone seen Erkala?"

No one answered. Kyp nodded to himself after a moment. "She'll catch up," he said and turned to Kym again. "So, how are your bunch doing?"

"For the first day out, I'd say good. Slow. There are some who haven't really flown in nearly a year. They're tired."

"But not you?" he asked.

"Not *me*?" she repeated and chuckled ruefully as she stretched her wings and lowered them. "Me most of all, unfortunately. I'm so out of practice I just want to tuck my head under a wing and sleep for three or four days straight."

Kyp glanced about. "And everyone else? How are you doing?"

"Tired," Kyf agreed.

"Tired and happy," Kyrt added.

"Hungry," I told him. "Are we going to talk long? The light's failing and I'd like to find some small portion of scavenge before it's totally gone."

"I don't want to keep you. I just wanted to chat for a few moments." Kyp adjusted himself on the branch and I could see that his talons were still sensitive after escaping the fire. "We're going to fly fast for the next few days. I want to start early and press hard. We'll only stop briefly to forage, and we'll fly until shortly before sunset. I'd like to leave as much ground as possible between us and the human's roost by the time those scouts make it back to Kuper and the Collection. So, with your permission, I won't stop for a real council until then."

General noises of agreement returned from throughout the tree.

"Then, unless you have anything you need to discuss, get yourself something to eat and find a comfortable roost. Safe — and comfortable," he added as an afterthought.

Everyone retired to forage except Kyp, Kyf and myself. Kyf waited until the others were gone, then hopped up closer to Kyp.

"It's going to be *very* hard for this bunch to fly any distance together," she observed.

Kyp cocked his head and peered at her. "Why?"

"Well," she said, turning a disapproving glance back at the various Crows spread out in the trees and on the ground. "Most of this flock are young. Slightly less than a quarter were freed from the human weaves just days ago. They barely know one another, let alone our bunch. Some barely speak the same language you and I do."

Kyp shrugged. "Kym seems to know how to communicate with them."

Kyf nodded. "And she's the *only* one. That's not a flock. That's a bunch of Crows who happen to be flying in the same direction, and not doing a great job at that. If everyone continues to fly on their own — in the same general direction, but essentially on their own — we risk losing individuals to owls, hawks, vultures. And if we can't communicate, truly communicate, well — we'll never become a real flock. And that's what you want, isn't it?"

"Yes. So, what do you suggest?"

"If it's all right with you, I'll talk some more with this Kym. I've had a chance to watch her and she seems smart — and of the ones who escaped from human confinement, she's the one who perches highest on the tree. Together, she and I should be able to set up teams that have individuals working with others they have never worked with. Let's mix things up a bit and get these new ones talking to others in the flock."

"It sounds like you know what you want," Kyp agreed. "Speak with Kym and set it up."

"Good," she concluded. There didn't seem anything more to say, but she lingered on the branch, picking at loose flakes of tree bark. "And one other thing," she added quietly.

"Yes?" Kyp's voice cracked and I could see the effort he was putting into presenting a calm exterior.

"It's about Kaf." She glanced over at the tree where Kaf was perched. "I miss Kwaku, but Kaf misses him more. He was easy around his brother in a way he isn't with anyone else. I've tried to help — but it's not the same. And it's not something we can talk about." She turned and gazed at Kyp. "Can you take care of him?"

Kyp nodded. "I'll try."

Kyf perched a moment as though weighing what had been said, then leaped from the branch. Kyp relaxed as she flew off. I was almost sorry to disturb him.

"There's one more thing," I said. He started as he realized he wasn't alone.

"Sorry," he apologized. "I didn't see that you were still there — I guess I'm not used to you being quiet. What is it?"

"That Kryk — the one you sent Kaf to talk with?"

"Yes. What about him?"

"I'm not sure what I'm saying, but ... you should keep your eye on him."

Kyp tilted his head to one side and scratched his throat. "Why?"

I searched for the words to express my feelings and finally blurted, "He's the most incompetent individual I've ever seen. That doesn't sound like something worth reporting. But it's a little astonishing just how truly useless he is. You've heard a bit about him. There are other things."

"Like what?"

"He makes noise at night in the roosts, for one thing."

"Noise?" Kyp stopped scratching. "What kind of noise?"

"A noisy kind — I don't know. Groans, moans. Grunts. Some of the others complained to me about it. I heard him recently, and it's unsettling. And it will attract groundlings to the roost. He won't keep up when we fly — he's always trailing. You know what Kyf's like — if someone has a problem, she can't resist helping. She hasn't told you, but she's flown about twice the distance you and I have because she keeps flying back to see if he's all right. And he's hopeless at foraging. You can see he's got a slight frame — I don't know if he's going to make it unless he eats something soon."

"Well, I'll try to offer some advice, and you can offer some, too. I'm sure spending time in confinement was hard on all of —"

I shook my head. "You're not listening. There's something else." I hesitated and then continued. "I didn't tell you this before. It didn't seem important at the time, and after, you were too badly hurt to consult. I freed him."

"In the human's roost?"

"That's right. Only, he wouldn't come out."

Kyp cocked his head. "He didn't come out of his weave right away?"

"No."

"Well," Kyp said, thinking back to the event, "maybe he was frightened by the fire."

"The fire hadn't started yet. He was one of the first ones I released."

"By all the noise and confusion, then."

"Maybe," I allowed, "but all the others came out easily enough. I had to chase him out."

Kyp stared at me. "*Chase* him out?"

"That's right."

Kyp turned to take in the tree where Kryk was perched. "So, what are you saying about him?"

"I don't know," I said at last. "I don't know what I'm worried about exactly. Just … I'd feel better if you kept an eye on him."

CHAPTER 3

We continued south, a westerly wind wrestling us with every flap we took. The fourth night, the snow turned to rain and it poured from then on. Not an on-and-off sort of rain but a frigid, relentless, water-up-your-beak variety. It sloshed down every moment we were flying and every moment we perched. If there had been more moments available, I believe it would have rained then as well. Crows that had lived along the coast maintained they were used to this kind of weather, but for myself, I prefer a dry flight, and I found it irritating.

We foraged the next day along the shore. Clams and mussels, mostly. The odd tiny minnow. Some of the yearlings picked at starfish. I don't know how hungry I'd have to be to attempt starfish but I wasn't there yet. I let them struggle away. A little disappointment can be character building.

Kyf became testy when she noticed that there wasn't proper watch kept while we ate. It wasn't so much that there wasn't a watch, but that there were two watches posted and neither performed its duty properly. That's when my eyes were opened to how much we still had to do.

The fifth day, Kyp called council, as he'd promised. In an attempt to get out of the worst of the wind and rain, we assembled in a thicket of gorse and bramble at the bottom of a rocky defile.

"Although the wind has been against us and the rain has slowed us down, we've made good time," Kyp began. "How's everyone?"

"Wet," I said as I shook my dripping feathers. "I'd be the happiest soul alive if I was a fish. Although," I added after a moment's thought, "I'm so hungry that if I was a fish I'd be tempted to eat myself."

Kyp chuckled. "Let's hope it doesn't come to that."

"Hey!" Kyf protested suddenly, snapping her head around to glare at me. "Why do you keep doing that?"

"What?" I asked a tad defensively.

"*Shaking* yourself?"

"Because I'm waterlogged. It's like a cloud has been trailing after me all day," I explained, "and emptied itself directly on my back."

"Well, take your miserable wiggle-waggle somewhere else," she complained. "I'm soaked enough without you performing your best wet-dog imitation."

"Kym?" Kyp called, cutting through our bickering. "How is your bunch doing?"

"Good. Tired. Wet."

"And Kyf?"

"Everyone's good. They're a little hungry."

"A little?" I repeated. "A *little*? If we're making good time it's because we're the lightest Crows that ever existed. There's nothing to us but feathers and an earnest desire to eat. Maker in the Roost, we have Crows who are taking after starfish. *Starfish* — that's just crazy desperation."

"I heard you speaking with Kyf earlier," Kyrt plunged in. "Are you talking about moving farther down the coast tomorrow, or tonight?"

"Both," Kyp replied. "I'd like to push on a bit now, after council, and then early tomorrow as well."

"Wait, wait, wait," I interrupted. "Let's return to the thing *I* was talking about. Eating. This isn't just about me and my appetite, so I'm not being entirely selfish. Almost everyone has said they're hungry, and some of these individuals were confined and had been refusing food from the human before we left their colony. If you don't let these Crows feed, they won't be able to fly later."

"The Collection," Kyrt objected, "won't be taking a day out to feed."

"How do we know that?" I demanded, then turned on him. "Don't roll your eyes at me! It's a reasonable question. We've seen a couple of their scouts. *They* didn't appear especially starved. I caught sight of that Kuper when he tried to recruit us. He seemed a pretty burly soul. You don't get that way without eating."

"My opinion," a low voice interrupted, "is we should go. And as quickly as possible."

We all turned and saw Erkala flutter to a branch.

"The faster we fly, the less likely to be seen. Rain is the Maker's special blessing. It will make it that much harder for others to catch our form and shade. And I suggest that when we forage, we forage where we are more easily hidden."

Kyp asked what all of us must have been thinking. "Where have you been?"

She adjusted her feathers. "Following the scouts."

A silence fell over the council.

"How far?" Kyrt asked.

"Till they arrived at the Collection."

Kyf cocked her head. "And?"

"Their flock turned north," Erkala replied.

A happy chatter erupted from the council.

"*Most*," Erkala interrupted. "Not all. Two bands separated out. One flew along the coast and south, the other south and west."

"How large were these bands?" Kym asked.

"Twenty, twenty-five each."

"Not so big," Kyrt observed.

"Big enough," Erkala argued. "Big enough to defend themselves and still send word back to fetch others."

"Did any follow you?" Kyrt asked.

Erkala sniffed scornfully and stared down her beak at the youngster. "Am I an egg? None saw me. I flew as no one else would have. The Collection was three, maybe four days' flight north and west from our roost. I have flown a day and half without stopping, not to roost, to rest or eat, to find you."

"You've said yourself that most went north —" Kyrt said, returning to his initial objection.

"Two things," Erkala said, interrupting him. "One, Kuper didn't wait. He sent his flock north right away — just what he'd do if he meant to intercept us. Two, he sent bands searching in different directions. If his first instinct proves wrong, these others are meant to catch us. Whatever else he wants — he wants us."

The council was digesting this as Kyp took up from where Erkala had left off. "The Collection is always searching for new members. We know that, so I wouldn't place too much regard on the bands Kuper sent out. If I understood what Kuper was saying when he spoke to us, they've been doing something like that since they formed. But I'm suggesting that Erkala is essentially right — not that we can't forage — but that we have to show caution. We should continue to fly hard. If we lose the Collection now and leave no trace, then the rest of our journey becomes much easier. If after six days the Collection finds nothing, they'll doubt. If after *sixty* days they have found nothing, they'll give up."

"They seem determined. What if they keep after us?" Kyf asked.

Kyp shook his head. "They won't. They can't. You heard Kuper back when he stopped us. He feels it's his duty to relay his supposed message from the Maker. That's what's important to him. He may dislike me —"

"He tried to *kill* you," I broke in, pointing out something I felt was obvious. "Twice. That's one way of expressing that you don't like someone —"

"He won't have time to chase us far," Kyp continued. "We're not that important."

"He sent scouts looking for us already," Kyf objected.

"That's different. I embarrassed him in front of his followers. But spring's approaching. Once winter is done, so is the Collection. It will scatter for nesting, just as every larger winter flock does. We only have to stay out of his way that long."

That seemed to make sense to everyone. When I really thought about the Collection, I could envision a few individuals who would remain with Kuper, but nothing of any consequence. Most of the Crows who flew with him were young and would already be thinking about places to erect nests.

"I have a question," Kym asked, "about something else. Is it safe to go back? What about the Plague? Are we likely to catch it when we return?"

Kyp didn't answer right away. "I don't know," he said at last. "I've already had a taste of it. You have. Kata and I flew some distance and didn't catch anything more. Everyone that flies with us now has either had it or been close to someone who had it. There doesn't seem to be any place free of it, so it seems to me that going back to our nesting grounds won't present a greater danger than going anywhere else. None of us caught it over winter. Maybe come summer we'll see another outbreak, but — I mean … we survived it last time. Perhaps that means we're free of it for good. I don't know. If it doesn't mean that …" He paused as though trying to find the best way to word it. "If it *doesn't* mean that, I don't know anywhere we can go that's safe."

On that disquieting note, the council broke. Some stayed for a short time to discuss things before they flew to look for food. Kyp accompanied Kym as she searched among the rocks.

"I doubt I'll find any snails," she admitted as she thrust her head into another crevice, "but I'd rather look and not find them here than look and not find them along the shore, with all those gulls and their racket."

"They're annoying," Kyp agreed as he poked about. "But can I ask you something that has been on my mind?"

"What?" she asked, her voice muffled within the surrounding rock.

"It would make sense if you were to become Co-Chooser."

Kym withdrew her head from the crevice. "Kyp, I can't."

"Ha. Found one!" Kyp said as he withdrew a tiny shell and cracked it against a rock. "Why not?"

"I haven't chosen anything for quite a time, for one thing. I spent many days. Many, many days when I didn't make the smallest decisions. Not about what I would eat, where I would perch, or anything really. That leaves me feeling a bit ... a bit —" she plucked a small leaf from her shoulder — "'weak' may be the wrong word, but let's say I don't feel confident right now."

"All the more reason to start making —"

"*And*," Kym continued, "a Chooser is Chosen. I haven't been. Half of the flock don't even know me. Got you!" she growled as she plucked a small snail from between two boulders.

"A third of the flock don't know *me*. Not really."

"But," Kym said, shaking her head, "they know that *you* freed them. That you found the human's roost. That you kept searching until you discovered a way to get us out. And they'll follow you anywhere because of that. And the others in this flock — they've flown with you, studied you, had a chance to take your measure. Kyp, I can help you to understand those ones who were in confinement with me, but I can't just Choose for the entire flock on your say-so. They would allow it — if you asked them to. I can't."

"Well," Kyp muttered, "that seems stubborn."

"Well," Kym said, prying a shell off a rock wall, "I am stubborn."

"Seems you could be a great help to me."

"You have my help," Kym demurred as she sorted through the shell fragments. "You don't need to make me Co-Chooser to get that."

"I suppose," he agreed, then continued more quietly. "There were other things we had discussed, before the Plague, about us. I don't have a food offering, but I could get one."

"Kyp, you don't think freeing me was an offering of a kind? And don't you know I accepted it already, but let's wait until —"

Some of the yearlings swept by at that moment, calling for help. Gulls had separated out three of our flock and taken that as a sign that we weren't prepared to defend them. The flock leaped up, and in a short time we'd driven the gulls off. No one was badly hurt, but some were bruised in the struggle.

It was just another disappointment in what had turned into a disheartening day all around. It wasn't the final disappointment, though. That was saved for later, when one of the yearlings announced the promising news that they'd found scavenge. I don't think I was the only one who felt their stomach stand up and take notice, but it turned out that the "forage" was skunk carcass — bad enough — but an already largely picked over and bony skunk carcass at that.

I foraged briefly, and without much enthusiasm, on some shriveled sumac berries that still clung to the branch. They made up for their brittle, bone-dry texture by releasing a bitter, faintly nausea-inducing aftertaste. The flock found roost in a cluster of crooked, slanting pines desperately clinging to a jumble of fallen rocks beneath a cliff overhang.

Rain continued to fall through the night. It would have been the second or third of the dark six when Kym dropped to the branch beside Kryk.

"What?" he asked nervously, glancing up.

"Why aren't you sleeping?" she asked in a calm, quiet voice.

"Sorry, I'm just restless," he explained.

"Anything in particular bothering you?"

"No, no," he said, shaking his head. "No."

"I was perched up there," she said, indicating with her head. "I noticed you were shivering."

"It's cold."

"And you were calling," she added.

"Oh?" he replied, glancing up as though gauging how far the branch was. "What did I say?"

"Help."

"Is that right? Did I say anything else?"

"No," she answered, and waited. "What were you dreaming about?"

"Oh, sorry, I don't remember. Dreams — they go as quickly as they come."

Kym shifted from one talon to another. "Anything you want to talk about?"

"No," he said, shaking his head again. "No."

"You're sure?" she inquired.

"Yes."

"You'll have to keep up."

"I will."

"All right."

Kym turned to go, but as she raised her wings to fly, Kryk said, "It's fine if you want to leave me behind."

She stopped. "Pardon me?"

"It's fine. I'd understand it. If I get too sick, or can't keep up. It's fine. Just leave me behind."

"Listen to me. Do you want to stay with us?"

"Yes."

"Then just keep flying. No one here is interested in leaving anyone behind."

The night closed about us, dark and silent. It had its secrets, as some in the trees had theirs. Let us stop to drink and stretch our wings, Cousins.

PART TWO

Draw in, Cousins. Is this wind chill? Does it stir your feathers and unsettle you? Take comfort that we have been colder. Are you still hungry? Do you wish there had been more time to feed? Take comfort that we have been hungrier.

I sometimes think every bad thing that happens is caused by hunger. Hunger makes you hasty. Hunger makes you grumpy. Hunger leads you to make decisions that you otherwise wouldn't. If we hadn't been hungry, maybe good sense would have prevailed.

But there it is. We were hungry. And when you're hungry, all you are looking for is the next good feed.

Cousins, settle in, find your place on a branch and listen. It seemed to me then, that although the weather grew increasingly warm, our difficulties grew worse. The damp, following the bitter cold, produced a persistent dry cough that spread through the flock. It wasn't serious, but it hampered us. And after experiencing the Plague the previous year, it worried us.

Still, Kyp urged us on, and Erkala was relentless. Were you the last as the flock flew? She had a reprimand. Were you late to leave feeding? She was behind scolding you.

Kryk received special attention because he continued to lag. When Erkala turned back for the third time that morning to reprimand him, Kyp intervened and instead offered a few words of encouragement.

Silently Erkala dropped back and flew alongside me. I heard her muttering darkly to herself, using the incomprehensible language she had first hatched with.

"I wouldn't upset yourself too greatly about this one," I advised her.

She peered grimly at Kyp and wagged her head. "He's wrong. The Maker doesn't mean our tests to be easy. Can Kyp be there to watch and help him all the time? No. Make this one take care of things, or life will take care of things for him, and life has a sharp bite and a quick temper."

Her tone was so bitter, I was a little taken aback. "Kyp is just trying to get us all to a safe roost," I reminded her.

"I know," she said, softening. "And for the most part he's fine. They" — she nodded back at the rest of the flock — "are certainly very fond of him. Maybe too much."

I looked at her curiously. "And you?"

She returned my glance. "Do you have to ask?"

And with that, she dropped to a lower level and spent the rest of the day's flight skimming just above the bushes and grasses.

The gulls had become such a constant nuisance we shifted inland to roost for the night. Kyp, always adept at finding a spot, discovered a tiny sheltered dale. Everyone broke into groups, as Kyf had organized them, with a few exceptions. Erkala and Kaf posted themselves at opposite ends of the valley, keeping watch, and I saw Kryk wander off on his own.

Later, as I searched for scavenge, I caught sight of him, poking about near the muddy, swirling floodwaters. The stream normally couldn't have been very impressive, but with the continued rain, it had spread well beyond its banks and found new places to run. I dropped to a soggy, fallen log, then scampered along till I found a projecting twig to perch on. I observed the youngster a few moments as he struggled to lift wet, heavy leaves and peered inside sodden woodpecker holes.

"What are you doing?" I asked at last.

He immediately straightened as though he had been caught in some kind of misconduct. "Just searching for food," he answered. That slightly startled expression was, I realized, something he carried with him most of the time.

I glanced about. There was almost nothing that looked even vaguely like food in the vicinity.

"Where?" I wondered aloud.

"Oh, I don't know. Yet. But I'm sure it's there," he gave a vigorous shake of his head that I suppose was meant to indicate determination. Or strength. Or deeper knowledge. Whichever. "I'll find some," he declared, followed by a resolute nod and a step forward, as though he was about to make off after something.

I peered along the opposite side of the log and looked up and down it. "Is anyone with you?"

He seemed uncertain about what I was asking. "Do you mean other than you?"

"Yes," I answered, as patiently as I could, "*other* than me."

"I don't" — he glanced upstream — "*think* so."

"Well," I began and felt my throat tightening.

Talking with him about even the simplest matters I found a special kind of emotional test. "You would *know* if someone was with you, wouldn't you?"

"Yes," he agreed. There was that nod again.

"So," I continued, trying once again to get things straight, "there's no one with you?"

"No," he answered, then peered up at me. "Sorry. Is that wrong?"

He seemed genuinely to be asking, so I applied restraint.

"Well," I replied, trying to keep my voice in check, "that's a good way of *becoming* food. You're next to a log, on the downslope side of the log. You can't see what's on the other side. You're at the bottom of a valley, so any groundling approaching from the eastern upslope side can see you. There's plenty of bush to provide cover if anything hungry and unfriendly wants to creep in close. You don't have anyone watching, offering protection or providing warning. *Where* are you from anyway?"

He stared at me blankly. "I was in that human roost that Kyp rescued."

"I *know* you were in that human roost!" I exploded. "I was there, too! I went in with Kyp and Kwaku and Erkala. Maker of the Maker, it was *me* who opened the weave you were in!"

"I'm sorry!" he exclaimed. "I remember you now. It was … smoky." He trailed off.

I paused, caught my breath, readjusted my feathers. It felt very undignified to lose my temper, but there was something about talking with Kryk that made me feel I'd been flying into a strong headwind all day. My wings suddenly felt heavy. "I'm asking where you were from *before* that."

"Before that? Oh, south of here."

"Then ... are we getting close to your territory?" A glimmer of hope seemed to present itself that he would soon rejoin his original flock.

"Oh, no," he said, nodding his head again. Did he always have to do that as though he was trying to dislodge a hornet? "It's south and west quite a ways. More south than west. But both. South and west. South, quite a bit, and then west, several days' flight."

"Oh," I replied, trying, unsuccessfully, to follow his directions.

"It doesn't matter, though," he added.

"No?"

"My Family was destroyed — nest, clan and flock — by the Plague."

"Is that right?" I asked, my spirits dropping. "Well, I'm sorry to hear that."

And there the conversation struck the limits of our imagination. Rain and running water filled the gaping silence. He stared at me earnestly. I reached down and plucked aside a loose piece of bark, revealing the rot underneath. "There. There's a cocoon. Try that."

"Thanks," he said and gratefully swallowed it.

I watched as this twitchy, scrawny Crow gulped this smallest morsel of food with such evident relish and realized how much more he would have to eat to develop any size or strength. And then I thought about how poorly equipped he was to find any food, or make his way in the flock, or do anything, really, and a wave of despair engulfed me. "I have to go," I concluded. "Forage somewhere safer. And don't eat at the bottom of valleys anymore unless you have someone watching. Do you understand?"

"Absolutely," he answered, nodding. Really, I worried that his head might roll off.

I flew away, and as I flew I knew that though I was hungry — starved, really — I would first have to nap just to recover from the exertions of that conversation.

CHAPTER 5

In the meantime, Kyp perched on a branch next to Kaf, who kept watch while others foraged. The flock was about evenly distributed between the ground and bushes, all quietly busy.

Kyp glanced about. "That's good to see. They're all eating."

"Looking for food anyway," Kaf allowed. "Not much selection here."

"No. There was more to be found by the shore. But there were the gulls."

"True," Kaf agreed, "there are always the gulls."

Kaf said nothing more than that, which wasn't unusual for Kaf.

"Are you tired?" Kyp asked after preening for a short time.

"No. A little, maybe. We're all tired, I suppose."

"Why don't you go on then?" Kyp suggested. "You should join the flock while they eat. Don't feel you have to take watch every time. Kyf and I will rotate the post."

"I don't mind doing my part. And Kyf won't give me work to do if I don't take it. She just wants me to perch with the others. *Roost* with the others. *Forage* with the others. Always wanting me to do *something* with the others."

"I think," Kyp suggested mildly, "she just wants you to talk with us sometime."

"What would I talk about?"

"What would you *talk* about?" The question took Kyp by surprise.

"Yes, what would I talk about? Kyf is always asking me if I've talked to anyone. So?" Kaf asked, "What would I talk about?"

"I don't know. Anything, I guess. You flew with Kwaku so long. It must feel strange for you to fly without him now. You might discuss things with others in the same way you discussed things with him."

Kaf didn't answer at once. When he began, it was in the same slow, soft voice he always used. "I see that Kyf's spoken to you. She thinks Kwaku and I talked all the time. Held long conversations that she wasn't part of, or that carried on after she left. The truth is, we didn't have to talk. He knew me. That's all, he just knew me."

Kaf scanned the horizon, glanced down at those foraging in a glade below. "You know, in my second year," he continued at last, "just after I'd come into my adult feathers, I was attacked by a hawk. It took me unawares and knocked me around pretty well. I barely escaped. The flock rallied in time and drove the hawk off, but I lost feathers in that exchange, from the middle of my back. It left a bare patch of skin about the size of a sparrow's head. Ugly to look at — and cold? I felt that hole every time the wind blew. Every time it rained. Every night as I perched just before sleep, I was aware of it. I was miserable and uncomfortable till I molted again and those feathers grew back in."

We hadn't gone far from the coast, and from the tree, one could see the ocean and gulls floating on the waves and circling in the sky, screeching. Even when Crows aren't there to screech at, gulls carry on. Kaf watched them rise and fall. "Kwaku's gone," he resumed, "and there's a wind that blows through that hole he's left in me. Now, you tell me, where's the molt that will replace him?"

He closed his eyes. When he opened them, he looked at Kyp. "Give me something to do. It isn't my intention to cause you or Kyf any worry."

Kyp considered the flock. "The yearlings have matured since they joined us, but there's lots they have yet to learn. They respect you. Can I ask you to watch over them? Provide advice for them. You don't have to say anything to them. Just be there if they have questions. Will you do that?"

"I will," he said, and nodded.

"And if you need anything from me, ask. Or," Kyp went on, "even if you don't need anything. I can't replace the hole you feel — maybe there's nothing that can — but there's always a space on the perch if you want it."

CHAPTER 6

Farther south, day after day. We continued flying as swiftly as we could. The rain followed us, whipped by a cold, blustery northerly. Along the coast we flew over a cluster of very active human colonies. Passing the human roosts always presented a contradiction. Everyone knew humans were dangerous, but equally, everyone knew some of the choicest scavenge could be found among them. Many of the scents that wafted up from human colonies were as poisonous, thick and cloying as a tern colony's, but humans also have a habit of presenting food in a way that can be very tempting. Frequently, when we flew over humans, enticing, aromatic hints of fruits and fish rose on the breeze.

We stopped outside one of the human's roosts along the coast and lingered long enough for the flock to forage through one of their caches. Kym and I perched in a tree as the rest of the flock scavenged.

I realized I hadn't really spoken much with Kym. She seemed without company, so I asked her, "How many of your folks still have the cough?"

She shook the rain off her back. "Ten. But they're all doing their best to keep up."

Like the rest of us, she was slight, and I thought I saw fatigue behind her eyes. "You were confined for a long time as well. Is it getting easier to fly?"

"Oh no," she answered and laughed, which seemed a surprising response. We hadn't, at this point, been a laughing sort of flock. "Harder, if anything. I'm more tired. I am surprised at how difficult it is, because I always loved flying. Now, my wings ache way past my shoulders into somewhere approaching my liver, I think. I keep thinking I should be able to carry my weight, but like the others I'm exhausted at the end of the day." And she chuckled again as though it was the funniest thing she had ever heard of. I found myself enjoying her company.

"I don't hear you complaining."

"And you won't!" she replied, and whetted her talons against the branch's soft, pulpy wood. "I am completely happy."

I glanced up to see if she was being sarcastic.

"I *am*," she repeated and then, seeing my lack of comprehension, continued. "You don't understand." She cocked her head, as though the explanation was to be found in the branch above her. "I had given up back there. Before you four entered the human's roost and released us? I had decided that *that* was the way the rest of my life would look. Confined. Only permitted to walk as far as the end of my weave. Never to perch in a tree again, never to smell leaves, or hear them whisper to one another in the breeze. Never to preen with others. I couldn't see how anything could possibly change that. So ..." She halted, then shrugged. "I can't believe I'm out here, with everyone. Every day, every moment, every wing beat is a lifetime I didn't expect to have. I'm exhausted from flying, absolutely. But I'm flying." She peered up at me. "That's a long-winded way of thanking you, I think."

"Thanking me?" I protested, suddenly embarrassed. "I wasn't looking for thanks."

"I know," she said, "which makes you that much more admirable."

I'm not sure that I had ever heard "admirable" used in any connection with me. I felt a rush of heat, and I believe I opened and shut my beak several times without saying anything.

Just then one of the humans' larger moving boxes rumbled closer, sparing me making a bigger fool of myself. It lurched to a halt, humans leaped out, grabbed their cache, flung it into the back of the box and then leaped in again. All of our folks jumped up and flew about, alarmed by the clatter and whir of the unexpected activity.

The moving box suddenly blasted smoke, roared and ambled into the distance, hauling away all the scavenge with them. And before I'd even had my turn to forage for the good stuff. It was with sadness and longing that I watched the moving box round a corner, but all at once I heard the same grumbling sound echoed, only much, much closer.

I turned and saw that, eerily, the sound was emerging from the black hole of Kryk's gaping beak. Sound for booming sound was repeated so precisely I had difficulty accepting that it was coming from him and not the humans and their things.

Some humans loping by below, apparently sharing my disbelief, grunted and gestured at us. Kryk's eyes flickered to the humans and in an instant he was imitating them as well.

"That's amazing," I said when he'd finished.

He wriggled with pleasure. I reflected how unused he was to receiving compliments. "I've always had a knack for repeating what I hear," he blurted.

"What else can you do?" Kym inquired.

He thought to himself, then his beak parted and he released the gruff, annoying *rar rar rar rar* of a smallish barking dog. He followed that with the trilling call of a lark, the calming hum and buzz of a hummingbird and the annoyed trill of a raccoon. By now he had drawn a slight crowd of our folk. "Something else," someone from the back called.

Kryk tipped his head to a side, considered a moment, then opened his beak. We froze. Kyf shot her head about and glanced sharply at us.

"What was *that*?"

Our stunned silence was followed by a burst of relieved laughter because we all knew too well what the sound was. We had heard it many times before — the soft, threatening (threatening partially *because* it's soft) call of a great horned owl. Even as we laughed, a slight chill ran through all of us to hear it.

"That was about the scariest thing I have ever heard!" enthused one of the youngsters.

"Oh," Kryk bubbled, almost pathetically happy to be receiving attention of a more positive kind, "there are scarier things than that." And all at once he had opened his beak and released a shrill note that tore through us, and suddenly I was seized and carried back in my mind to the dark, sweltering human roost, when the fire clawed at my throat and black smoke choked us. I felt the same gut-wrenching fear

I had in the human's roost when the high-pitched wail of the roost had shrieked and flames had consumed everything.

"Stop!" I shouted, horrified. "Stop that! Stop!"

"Sorry," Kryk apologized quickly and closed his beak, embarrassed. The silence that followed was complete.

"Nest of the Nest," Kyf snapped as she flew up beside him, "what's *wrong* with you? We're trying to move south as quietly as possible, and you go and do a thing like that —"

I raised a wing to calm her. "Wait. Did you see how the humans reacted?"

CHAPTER 7

There was scavenge to be found along the shore, but increasingly, there was the troubling matter of the gulls. They were loud, relentless, and there were thousands of them. If you took an interest in a beached fish, four or five gulls dropped next to you. If you plucked up a clam and dropped it onto the rocks, before you could retrieve any flesh, the gulls were there. If our flock went down in force, the sky above us filled with flailing wings and shrill gull calls.

Time and again, we were chased off one site after another. And the gulls grew more insistent and belligerent with each success.

In an effort to show some initiative, I pinched a mussel from a fat, distracted gull, then had to fly nearly to the beginning of time and back to keep three of his gull companions from retrieving it. When I finally did crack it open, there was so little flesh that I was hungrier after eating it than when I'd begun. I discarded the splintered remains with disgust.

"What's wrong with what we're doing?" I asked, prying a sticky splinter of shell from my right wing and flinging it down.

"Nothing," Kyp replied, shaking his head tiredly. "Just the wrong spot. The wrong spot, and a little too much gull. It's getting late, let's move off the coast, find ourselves a comfortable roost inland and forage for a little while."

We retreated west until we'd found a stand of oaks to collapse in. We were all tired and irritable. Some had stopped coughing but were still weak. Others had just caught the sickness and were dreading the days ahead. As we sat on the branch, I listened to the painful rasps and wheezes repeated through the trees and considered our gloomy surroundings.

"I don't mean to complain —" I began at last.

"Good," Kyp grunted. "Don't."

"But is it wise to keep going south?" I persisted.

"We have to go far enough," Kyp explained slowly, as though addressing a fledgling, "that the Collection won't believe we could have gone that far."

"Well. *I* can't believe we've gone this far."

Kyp glared up from his preening. "Is there a problem?"

"No one knows this terrain," I pointed out.

"I led everyone here. I'm going to lead everyone out."

"I'm not questioning your leadership, I would never question that. Everyone knows you are the only one sufficiently crazed to keep this bunch together. What I'm questioning is your ability to keep me adequately fed. No one knows where to forage or find food. *You* can fly on nothing but the vague memory of a meal. I admire that in a strange kind of way — and congratulate you on that — but I require something a bit more regular. I'm more of the sort who needs to eat every day. Sometimes several times a day. So tell me, how far south will we go?"

"As far as we need to."

"Oh, well," I said archly, "that tells me everything."

"It's getting warmer as we move south. I would have thought you'd be happy. Do you have a *problem* with warmer?"

"'Course I don't have a problem with warmer. But this is already so far outside my territory, I don't know which way is up — and we've got Crows from all over and this is outside *their* territory. We're competing with gulls and terns and plovers and some things I've never heard of. I'm not sure what to eat and what not to eat. I saw a snake yesterday, bigger than I've ever known existed, and a day ago there was some kind of lizard thing in the water that swallowed a heron, and I mean it just swallowed it in one gulp, and all I'm asking is how much farther?"

"As far as we need to," Kyp repeated frostily. And stared.

I returned his stare, frost for frost. "You're a very difficult Crow to talk to," I told him after a moment.

"I know," he answered shortly.

"*Very* difficult," I repeated.

We perched there. Someone else coughed. The wind lifted my feathers, permitting more rain and damp under. I smoothed them, realigned them and peeked up at Kyp. He was perched facing into the rain and wind, water streaming down his beak and dripping off his shoulders.

"Things were a lot easier when it was just the two of us flying together," I sighed. "Remember that?"

"Yes."

"That seems like a long time ago. I warned you then. I warned you the moment Kyf, Kaf and Kwaku came along and asked to join us. I told you then things would begin to get difficult."

"You did," he agreed, and nodded.

"Now you miss those times, don't you?"

"You always talked too much. I had to invite others into the flock just so there would be someone else to share the demanding listening duties."

His tone was light, but he looked tired, and I could see him favoring his good leg as he rested.

"So," I said finally, "when Kwaku appeared in my dream after the fire, he told me that you would need my help. How can I help?"

"This territory is different, you're right. And it's strange for all of us, but if anyone knows foraging, it's you. The yearlings could use your advice and assurance about where to feed."

"It's not advice they need," I disagreed. "It's time. I'm not trying to be difficult. It's just not possible for all these individuals to really forage, in unfamiliar surroundings, in the time we're giving them. You're pushing them too hard. I appreciate that we have to travel fast, but there are other considerations."

"There's been forage along the way…"

Kyf hopped down from the higher branch where she had been perching. "Excuse me, I couldn't help overhearing. Much as I regret it, I agree with him." She nodded, a little distastefully, in my direction. "For the distance we've been flying, and the speed we've been going, we haven't stopped to feed long enough. Just look at us — we're all thinner. And you," she said rounding on Kyp, "should be taking better care of yourself. What do you think the quality of your feathers will be when they finally come back in if you don't get the food you need now?"

Kyp shook his head. "You keep talking about speed, but we haven't been flying that fast. If we're being followed, it would be possible — easily — to catch up with us. We saw that with Erkala."

Kyf shook her head. "For the condition this flock is in, it's been very fast. And it will always be easier for an individual to fly faster than a group. And Erkala is, as we all know, a very unusual and determined Crow."

"And we would fly much better," I said, returning to my theme, "if we had a decent feed."

"I agree with you both, that it would be better if we had something more to eat, but you eat what you find, and we've all had our eyes open. We've all been looking. What can we do? We have to wait until something comes to us."

I glanced at Kyf. "Maybe we can do a little better than that."

Kyp turned to me and squinted. "What did you have in mind?"

CHAPTER 8

We flew in along the coast, deep into a narrow inlet I'd scouted earlier. There, on either side of the inlet, a number of humans perched on their bobbing, floating boxes. I wondered again, as we flew overhead and saw some humans submerged in the water and others running along the beach, if the humans that live on the ocean are different from the ones that live on land. They seem a livelier bunch. It's not unlike the difference between the turtles you see swimming, scrambling and rooting in swamps and the tortoises you see in the dry lands — who essentially just sit there. There's something about water that seems to stimulate.

We flew farther inland and came to the end of the inlet. "There it is," I said.

The humans had erected a long, low wooden structure, like an enormous nest of piled logs that projected deep into the bay. At the landward end of this structure they had constructed a wide, squat roost with colorful skins that stretched out and up from it. In the shade of these stretched skins, they had arranged various things fetched up from inside their floating boxes: coils of coarse vine, piles of fruits and berries — and stacked within containers of shattered ice were heaps and heaps and heaps of shiny, delicious-looking fish.

"There are a lot of things down there," I told Kyp. "Things I'm guessing are fruits, others ... well, I'm not sure what they are. But the fish. The fish, I *know* are good to eat."

"Why do you think they do that?" Kym asked as we watched the humans stalk through the stacks of fish and fruit.

I was so taken by the enticing vision and aromatic smells that I hadn't really given her my full attention. "Pardon me?"

"Lay their food out like that," she said, craning her head to look below. "They're not *eating* it."

I gazed again at the rich array of food in front of us. Fish of all kinds and sizes lay spread out in the open or submerged in water-filled containers.

"Is it prayer? Or is it display?" she wondered aloud. "Some birds do something like that."

I eyed the humans attending to their salvage. "A prayer I could understand," I agreed. "Humans have a lot to atone for. But display? For whom?"

"For each other?" she speculated.

"Each day? It doesn't make any sense to me."

"It's the human, Kata —"

"And *that* means it doesn't have to make sense. Yes, I know."

"Although," Kym mused, "I'm sure that it all means something. Something. If we could only figure it out."

"But understanding what that something is will have to wait upon another day," Kyp interrupted. "Everyone has gathered and we want to use this daylight. Let's get organized."

In a short time, our flock was hidden in the trees and bushes lining the inlet. Kryk was situated on top of the squat, sprawling human's roost, above the heads of the humans and well out of their sight. He had selected for his perch the mouth of a small smooth tunnel the humans had fashioned from a thin kind of stone. As he clambered into it, his talons made light scratching noises. He turned about, settled and was still. He nodded to me.

"Ready?" I called.

From around the inlet, I received subtle visual signs of everyone's readiness. I glanced over at Kyp, who nodded as well. I raised my wings once, and Kryk opened his beak.

Suddenly the air was shredded. Hearing that high-pitched, warbling cry made me shudder. When I glanced over at Kym and Kyp, I could see it had the same unnerving effect upon them. Only Erkala appeared unmoved by it.

If it upset us, it nearly made the humans lose their minds. Below us on the ground they suddenly leaped up and raced about, gathering in tight bunches to shout, glancing this way and that, then running again. Pointing. Calling to one another. Frantic.

Abruptly another noise split the air. I peered at Kyp, who leaned in and told me this had been his addition to the plan. Kym had confided to him that she was capable of imitating the sound of those moving boxes with twirling lights on their heads. They, Kyp told me, had some kind of special effect on humans.

It must have been true, because if the previous sound had frightened the humans, this new sound proved too much. They swarmed out of their roost and ran, climbing over one another in their efforts to get away. In a few moments, the space below was abandoned.

I glanced at Kyp. "Care to eat?" I asked.

He nodded, called to the others, and we all swept down into the human's roost.

Inside, it was dark and cavernous. Row upon row of fish lay draped on flat surfaces, piled high in stacks, immersed in glittering pools of water. The choices presented! Great Crow in the Nest, the number, the size and the colors of fish that were displayed. I wouldn't have thought the Maker had made that many varieties. A quick glance revealed many of our folk quietly, fixedly gorging themselves. One of those released from the human's roost was so overcome by the quantity of delectables offered that she simply spun around and around and around in one spot, her beak agape. Another, figuring it was better to select a single fat fish than several smaller, had seized a snapper twice his size and was dragging it laboriously across the ground by its tail.

"Everyone!" Kyp called sharply over the tumult. "Good eating! And the best we've ever had. But the human will return in no time! So take what you want, but be quick."

That got us moving. Everyone hurried to select a treat they could carry away. Although I understood the need for haste, I couldn't help myself. A heaping pile of sweet, glistening squids spilled to the ground near me, daring me to pass them by. I stopped to sample one, had another and then a last one for good luck. I must have got caught up in the event, because before I could collect my scavenge all together, I realized that, as Kyp had warned, the humans were returning — and they weren't happy. I hopped to my right, grasped a sleek, slippery fish — a red-skinned, wide-mouthed fellow nearly as big as myself — and flew off.

Kyp had been skipping from one place to another, urging our famished cousins to hurry, when suddenly a tall, hairy, angry-looking human scrambled around a corner. Its eyes bugged out of its head as it caught sight of the disturbance, and with a wild cry it lunged at Kyp, who leaped to the top of a flat surface. Apparently it was slipperier than he had understood, and instead of lifting off, he stumbled, landed hard on his chest and slid along that surface like an otter slithering down a muddy bank. He shot off the one surface, bumped onto another and stopped only long enough to seize a purple crab from a stack near him. Then he hopped into the air with the crab clutched in his talons, looped back at the human, which was still chasing him — hooting and shaking its fleshy paws — and Kyp released that crab, directly, immediately, forcefully upon the upturned face of that very surprised human.

Then, with a neat little twist and somersault flourish, he spun about and swooped in low over the same flat surface I had initially foraged at. He lowered his talons, nabbed himself a handsome yellow and blue fish head — and was gone.

Then it was out of the roost, out of the human's grasp and out, out, out under the welcoming open sky again! It was such artistry, such craft of flight, such skill from the very beginning of his escape to the inspired choice of the correct crab to fling, to the neat little twist and roll at the end that a loud, happy cheer spontaneously erupted from the entire flock. Congratulating ourselves through our full beaks, we flew from there like the wind itself, laughing as we went. I glanced about and saw that there was no one in the flock who wasn't flying laden with some delicious morsel or another.

At last we settled in a quiet grove near a slow-moving stream, considerably heavier now than when we had set out earlier in the day. A special satisfied kind of silence fell over the glade as everyone set about the serious business of feeding.

I saw Kyf and Kaf happily hunched over a cluster of tiny purple and gray herring. Kryk had fetched back a long, thin eel that was more bone than anything else, but his value had risen so greatly in the past few moments that others were more than eager to share with him. He chatted cheerfully with two or three others as he plucked at the assortment piled in front of him. On a branch high up to my left, Kym perched with a drooping octopus dangling from her beak. I glanced over at Erkala, who, already finished dining on flounder, was picking her talons clean and whetting her bill against a rock.

"Good eating like we haven't seen in some time," I commented between bites. I'll admit I was at least partially reaching for a compliment. It had, after all, been my idea.

Erkala nodded stiffly. "Very good eating," she agreed. "Very good. But if any other birds were watching — they will remember the size of our flock, the way we flew and that our Chooser was a Crow who could fly like no other. We might as well have shouted from the tops of the trees that we were here." With that she raised her wings and flew to the crest of a pine to keep watch.

I kept eating — I wasn't going to let anything interfere with that — but the fish didn't taste quite as good as it had before.

CHAPTER 9

I left something out.

When we swept through the human roost and stole all those lovely fish, I couldn't resist one other tiny, indulgent extra theft. A human had left a tempting circular glitter lying about, thin as a hummingbird's beak, perfectly round and irresistibly shiny. I'd already selected my fish, but I took that one moment more to slip my head through the glitter and shrug it down around my shoulders. As I flew away, I couldn't help but wriggle a bit with pleasure.

Of course, as we flew away, everyone noticed. I became the object of much interest — and perhaps even a little jealousy — and received many, many compliments. But as we continued to fly, there was no question but the glitter was a nuisance. It rubbed and chafed. It caught on twigs and choked me whenever I perched. It drew attention — unwanted, dangerous attention — from birds outside our flock. And as I tired of carrying it, I realized I couldn't simply cache it somewhere and come back for it later. We weren't, after all, intending to return this way. A wiser individual than I would have recognized the hazard it presented and discarded it without a second thought. In fact, Kyp noticed that I seemed uncomfortable carrying it and urged me to drop it.

If only things were that simple.

The truth was that although I'd initially plucked the glitter up on a whim, without any special plan, somewhere along the way as we flew I began to develop a vain and reckless idea, so vain and so ill considered that I was ashamed to even share it with anyone. It was my arrogant and empty notion that when Kyp finally led us home, when we arrived at our Gathering Tree at the end of what would certainly be many, many days of hard flight, I would be permitted to glide to the top of the Gathering Tree and slip that delicate circlet around the topmost branch as an offering. A symbol of our efforts and trials throughout this long, long journey.

Which just shows how small my dreams were. Kyp was busy every moment planning how best to get us to our roost safely. I was simply thinking about how pleasant it would be if everyone admired me. But there you go — you dream what you dream. I pressed on, and the glitter shimmered, chafed and reproached me as I flew.

The next day, in the fifth sixth, I noticed two Crows — Kyrt and Kyl — returning to the flock, flying full out. I slowed to learn what the trouble was. I didn't have to wait long. "We've spied a band of Crows," Kyrt gasped as he pulled up beside me.

Kyp quickly joined us. "Where?"

"Not far. Inland a short flight." Kyrt gestured to Kyl. "*He* says he recognized them."

Kyl nodded. "I saw some of them in the Collection."

"You're sure?" Kyp demanded.

"Yes," he replied. "One of them was the scout we captured, Kyup."

"How many in the band?" I asked.

"Twenty. Twenty-one."

Kyrt turned to Kyp. "What should we do?"

Kyp thought a moment. "And you're certain you weren't seen? Neither of you?"

Kyrt shook his head. "No one saw us."

Kyp adjusted his feathers as he thought.

"Everyone's tired," Kyp said finally. "All we're going to do is take a nice little rest. And perch very quietly. There." And he nodded in the direction of a distant group of tiny islands out beyond the breakwater.

It was drizzling and gray when we arrived at the island. The sun had slipped into a bank of rising mist. The surf pounded, and the wind coiled in and among the trees, hissing softly. We perched and rested among a stand of long-needled pine. The night fell quickly and completely, a giant lid closing over the eye of the day.

As night deepened, the wind dropped. There wasn't much discussion in the roost, we were that tired. Early in the dark six, a fuss rose on the other side of the tree. Kyf fluttered to a spot close beside Kyp. "They're saying someone heard something."

Kyp raised his head. "Heard what?"

"They don't know."

"They don't know?" Kyp repeated, puzzled. "Can anyone tell what it sounded like?"

Then I heard it, too. Out in the rain, beyond the trees. Something sweeping by.

I squinted into the night. Of course, I couldn't see a thing. Without stars or moon or human lights, the darkness was nearly absolute — and with the constant drip of the rain through the branches and hiss of the wind, it was impossible to determine for sure what you were hearing either, or if you were truly hearing anything.

And yet? I tipped my head forward. If I con-centrated ...

"There," I said. "I heard something go past."

"Me too," Kyp whispered.

I turned to Kyp. "What did *you* hear?"

"I don't know yet." Kyp stepped closer to Kyrt and spoke in a hushed voice. "I want you to drop down through the tree. Spread the word that everyone is to stay close to the trunk, as close as they can. Shift along the perch to the center of the tree. If they feel crowded, that's probably good. You understand?"

"Yes," he replied and dropped to the branch below. Kyp turned to Kaf.

"You do the same," he directed, "only take the top of the tree."

Kaf said nothing, just spread his wings and spiraled up alongside the trunk.

We perched, listening. Kyp craned his neck. "There," he whispered, hearing it again.

I nodded. There was another movement somewhere just beyond the branches.

Suddenly voices erupted near the bottom of the tree. Kyrt returned, his feathers bristling.

"What is it?" Kyp demanded.

"A body's been found near the base of the tree," he breathed.

"Of who?" I asked.

"We don't know yet." He gulped. "We couldn't tell."

"Couldn't tell? What condition is the body in?" I asked.

Kyrt lowered his voice even more. "His head's been taken off."

Kyp skipped closer to Kyrt. "I want you to go back down. Tell everyone to keep quiet and stay close, feather close. It's very important. Whatever they hear, they are *not* to fly out beyond the branches. *Not*. Now go."

Kyrt flew off. I listened intently. "An owl."

"That's right," Kyp agreed, absently. "It's a perfect night for them." Kaf reappeared and I told him what we'd just heard.

Kyp interrupted my explanation. "Kaf, go back up. Tell the others that they have to be prepared. They're to keep watch for one another. To do that, they'll have to stay quiet. If they're attacked, they'll have to leap in right away. But they can't fly out beyond the branches. In the dark, beyond the tree, they'll lose their sense of direction and the owl will have every advantage. Tell them."

Again, Kaf waited patiently until Kyp had finished his instructions, then disappeared into the upper reaches.

Moments later a clamor of shrill voices erupted.

I turned in the direction of the sounds. "It's up top."

I listened. Voices in a panic. Wings sweeping out in the darkness. My heart sank. "Maker of the Maker," I muttered, "some of the flock have left the tree."

"The owl will take as many of them as it wants out there," Kyp said quietly, then spread his wings. "I'm going to see what I can do."

I placed a talon on him. "What can you do?"

"I don't know. Get them to return to the roost."

"I'll come," I said.

"Don't," he ordered. "*You* have to stay here. If others fly out, it will be able to pick us off. I need someone to keep the flock organized. I'll see what I can do."

Suddenly I heard a loud voice calling over the panicked cries, trying to calm the others.

"It's Kaf," Kyp said shortly and leaped off the branch.

The rain, the dark, the mist made it impossible to see anything. The rain, the tide and the wind made it next to impossible to be heard.

"Be quiet!" Kyp called to the yearlings who were milling about, but he was interrupted as a searing flash of light split the sky. In that brief flash, I saw Kyp and Erkala frozen amid a million glittering drops of rain. The light disappeared. An explosion of thunder followed.

"I told you," Kyp snarled, catching sight of me, "to stay back. Now the owl can simply take as many of us as it wants, and no one will maintain order. *Please*. Go back. Convince the others to stay put."

"I know where the yearlings have flown!" Erkala shouted over the rain and then grunted. Simultaneously I felt a massive figure brush silently past, throwing me off balance. I turned, flailed at the darkness and heard the owl's harsh hunting cry sound nearby.

Lightning crisscrossed the sky again. There was Erkala beside me. Kyp above us and to our right.

"Ow," Erkala complained. "That's *me* you're hitting."

The darkness closed around us again, and the thunder trailed away.

"Sorry," I apologized. "I saw that you're cut. How badly are you hurt?"

"The owl cut me along the back," Erkala said matter-of-factly. "I twisted just before it struck and missed the worst of it. It must be flying through us, taking Crows as it goes past."

"Help me call to the others," Kyp shouted, "and let's guide them back to the tree! There's nothing anyone can do out here. We're all lost in this Maker-stricken darkness. In the tree we at least have some branch coverage and will be able to orient ourselves better."

After the brilliance of the lightning, the darkness seemed more absolute than ever. We flew cautiously. Suddenly Kyp grunted, and I felt him brushed aside. Erkala gave a short yelp of pain, then shouted, "Just go!"

Lightning cut the sky again. There was Kaf a few wing strokes away. Kym, frozen, below us. And there, atop Erkala, the massive form of a great horned owl spread, eyes blazing, talons stretched, beak agape. Kyp threw himself on its back, hoping to disable it or drive it off. The light flickered and disappeared. Thunder followed, drowning out our cries.

Through that thick darkness, I felt more than saw a tumbling ball of owl and Crow bodies revolve and twist as it dropped through space. Cries of pain, groans of exertion and shouts of encouragement emerged from the squirming mass. Finally it hit the ground with a soggy, ominous thump.

Stunned, we all lay there amid the wet dirt and pine needles, gasping. The wind briefly blew the clouds aside, allowing a shaft of moonlight to illuminate the landscape. In horror, we stared as the immense form of the owl began to slowly rise. Kaf leaped up, calling to the rest of us. "Don't let it leave the ground!"

He was right, of course. As long as the owl remained earthbound, we held the advantage. The moment it lifted, it could slip back into the thick folds of darkness and return to kill us, one at a time.

Now we played a grim version of tag. The owl shrugged Kaf off, and Erkala jumped in. She was tossed aside and I flung myself at it. Kyp and Kym followed. There were times when it was impossible to tell who was in and who was out. Grunts and screams covered any other sound. Every time one was thrown off, another climbed on top.

And then all at once it was quiet, broken only by the soft persistent hiss of wind slithering over sand and the monotonous tapping of rain. A black silhouette lifted and I drew in a breath.

"Erkala?" I whispered after a moment's pause, "Is that you?"

"Yes," she wheezed, and I realized she must have taken a hard hit to her chest.

Another form rose, close beside me.

"Kata?" Kyp asked as he stood.

"I'm right beside you," I answered.

"Kym?" he called.

"Yes," she replied shakily, regaining her talons and standing.

"Kaf?" I hollered.

No reply.

"Kaf?"

Nothing.

CHAPTER 10

Grief needs its own time to breathe. The next day we spent the first sixth in mourning, for Kaf and the three others the owl took, Kympt, Kyl and Keflew. Then as light gradually warmed the trees in the second sixth, we flew west.

The flight was a subdued one. There was little talk, and it seemed to me right that we spent the day quietly. Kaf was someone who wasted no time talking. I never heard him say anything bad of anyone. He never complained. He didn't argue. He was one of those who quietly took care of the things that have to be looked after when other folk, like myself, are still chattering. It was typical that he would have flown out to help the yearlings without saying anything — if something had to be done, he just did it. It was like him that he would die first. He was the type who would scout ahead for the rest of us. And of course it was typical that he would have joined Kwaku. They had always been inseparable.

These and other sad thoughts possessed me as we flew. We passed over the strait that had separated us from the mainland. Soon we had abandoned the coast and, for the first time as a flock, we continued inland until the smells and sounds of the ocean receded and finally disappeared.

Kyp didn't give any direction or provide a reason for why we had turned west. No one asked.

The fog remained thick over the land as we flew. After the attack by the owl, there was some anxiousness about traveling through it, but Kyf was able to reassure the yearlings. Since our flight from the human's roost, they had come to rely upon her more and more for guidance.

Thinking that this might be a time when Kyf would want to be left a bit to herself, I steered in her direction and tried to offer a little help, but she dealt with them efficiently, as she always did, and sent them away more at ease. After, she looked at me witheringly. "What?" she asked. "Are you worried that I've suddenly become incompetent?"

"No," I assured her.

"That I'm not *able* to carry out my duties?"

"That's not it at all," I protested. "You are completely able. If I offer help, it's not because I think you have a failing."

Kyf glanced at me. "You don't think so?"

"No. You are ..." I tried to find the correct words to reassure her and let her know just how much everyone relied on her. "... very strong. Very, very strong. Everyone sees that."

She didn't reply for a while, and then said, "I know how to organize a flock. That's true. And I've managed to convince those young ones that we won't come upon another owl right away — although we might. I can't see anything in this mist. But both my brothers have died now, and I wasn't there to help them because I was too busy with others. Doesn't that strike you as a bit of a serious flaw?"

She flew ahead. I called after her, but she ignored me, and I realized that there would be nothing I could say or do at this time that would make any difference. Maybe when the pain was less fresh.

We had started our day late, and so the flight wasn't a long one. Still, the efforts of the previous days had taken their toll and, once everyone finally found roost, we fell asleep quickly.

My sleep was troubled. I dreamed, and woke, only to dream again. Sometime early in the dark six I woke from a dream that had been replaying. I was in an argument with Kaf and was telling him that there was too much to do and he couldn't leave, and then somehow the dream changed and turned into someone else arguing, and then I discovered someone else *was* arguing. I was awake. It was the middle of the night. Hushed voices could be heard bickering out at the edge of the roost.

"There *is* another choice," the first low voice maintained.

"What choice is that?" asked the other.

"There are enough of us here that we could attack them." And now the other voice became clearer. It was Erkala.

"We can't risk it," someone said — Kyp, I realized. And I could see him in my mind shaking his head.

"Look at the risks we're taking now."

"If even *one* escaped and flew back, then the rest could be counted on to follow."

Erkala's voice, already quiet, became even quieter. "Then we would have to make sure that none escaped."

"And how would we do that? And how many would *we* lose? The ones who were confined by humans are barely in shape to fly, let alone fight, and the rest of this band are inexperienced. How many would be injured? And then what? Do we battle each group again, each time we meet? I mean to get away from here and find a new start for those who have chosen to follow me. If I lose Crows and return to our nesting grounds with wounded and maimed companions, I'll have failed."

"We have a distance to go. And all that may happen no matter what you choose."

I shifted on the perch to listen better, but they must have heard me because their voices dropped. One of them hushed the other, and I heard no more.

CHAPTER 11

Early the next day, noise awakened me. At first I
thought it was Erkala and Kyp arguing again, but as
I opened my eyes I heard it once more. Up the
valley, a faint wail broke the silence, swelling, then
lowering into a wet, ragged sputtering. Kyf
dropped to the branch next to me.

"What do you think that is?" she asked, peering
through the vapor.

"I think I'm sick of this fog, is what I think," I
grumbled. "You can't see anything. You can't tell
what's doing what. How long has that noise been
going on?"

"Don't know. I heard it earlier. Two, maybe three
times. It starts, stops, starts again."

There it was once more, eerily, cutting through the swirling haze, rising and slipping into a broken cry as though bubbling up from somewhere deep beneath the water.

"There's definitely something down there." That was Kyp, just up and over from me in the roost.

"What, though?" Kyf inquired. "Owl?"

"Whatever else that is," Kyp observed, "it's not owl."

"At least not the kind of owl we've heard before," Kym corrected him. She'd joined us as well.

"This is so far out of our territory it could be any-thing," Kyrt said as he dropped to a branch beside Kyf. The noise was unsettling everyone. "Maybe it's not something that would come with any territory," he added. We turned to look at him.

"What do you mean?" Kyp asked.

"There are some muttering that ghosts have fol-lowed us," he confessed. "Spirits of those who died from the Plague."

"Why would *ghosts* come?" Erkala snorted, and I saw that she had silently landed beside me.

"Angry. That's what some say," Kyrt answered. "Upset that we didn't make the flight with them to the Maker."

"That's nonsense," Kym replied softly, "although everyone thinks that at some time or other."

I squinted into the mist. That sound, like a raw voice, rising and falling. "I don't know that ghosts would have the stomach for following us," I said. "A little too much flying for ghosts. My understanding is the dead are allowed a little rest."

"My understanding is the dead," Kyp replied, cocking his head and listening intently, "don't complain as much as the living."

"Of course they don't. They're *dead*. Those of us who are still alive, though —"

"Is it possible it's the Collection?" Kyf interrupted with a frustrated toss of her head.

"The Collection?" Erkala repeated, and we all listened. She clacked her beak dismissively. "That voice tastes something of Crow — but if the Collection arrives, I don't think it will announce itself to us."

"It may be Crow, it may be ghost, but either way I can't understand *anything* it's saying," Kyf said after a moment, then turned to Kym. "Can *you* understand it? You have the most skill with accents."

We listened harder. A wheezing cough broke the silence, startling us, and Kryk's rasping voice hissed up to us "*Sorry!*" Suddenly Kym jumped up and flew ahead to a bush situated a little lower in the valley. The sun slowly began to emerge through the mist, carving long jagged shadows, like immense orange talons reaching through the tree trunks.

"It seems to me," Kym said slowly, "mostly to be … curses."

And she was right. Once you heard it, it was obvious. Within the rising and cresting pattern of the voice, it was possible, if one listened closely, to make out the occasional well-placed curse in a call that was a long stream of words run together.

"Well, we won't find out what it is from here," Kyp said at last. "Kyf, take the flock south and west. If we fall into trouble and don't catch up right away, double back and we'll meet at the hill with the skinny sycamore."

She nodded and returned to the flock.

The rest of us flew cautiously over the winding river. Trees sagged and tilted along its banks. A turtle dropped from a flat rock and sank out of sight. Mist coiled and skidded over the water's surface, then rose in feathery swirls. The voice, or voices, grew louder.

Then, as we skimmed the tops of rushes in the reeds almost directly below us, we heard a sudden, jarring splash, followed by a long, scalding spurt of oaths.

"Maker of the Maker, I'm ..." the voice raged before fading away into bubbles. "Mites in the Nest, is there no one with the ability to *hear*?" it erupted again, snarling. More curses. I examined the bushes all about, but still saw nothing. A heavy panting rose from deeper in the tall grass and soggy under-growth. We landed as quietly as we could, then sloshed slowly to our left. The scummy gray-green water lapped about our bellies, and slick mud oozed between our talons.

"Watch for snakes," Erkala cautioned quietly. "This is the kind of place they like best."

"You want more? I'll give you more!" the voice fumed, clearer now. "You think I'm afraid of you? Brood of the First Brood, I'm no more afraid of you than I am afraid of that first bunch you sent." That was followed by a tremendous thrashing, then still more cursing.

"If it's a ghost, it's a ghost with a very broad ..." — Kym mused — "... vocabulary. There're things being said all in one breath that I haven't heard most Crows say in a lifetime."

Kyrt spiraled up to a branch overlooking the valley, to keep watch as we proceeded. I glanced back at Kyp, as I came upon the bodies of two dead Crows lying along the bank. I separated the long grass ahead of us and carefully peered under a log that was half submerged.

There I saw him. A large, very aged Crow in a terrible state. He was muddy — more than half his body was caked in the thick, sticky clay. He was bloody — one eye was closed and oozing from a cut. There were primaries missing or snapped on both wings. Another looping cut along his neck had dried in a red and angry line. He was wedged beneath the log, his neck craned at an awkward angle as he struggled to keep his beak above the sludge. When I peeked in, he glared at me with his good eye.

"Good eating," I greeted him.

He responded with another lengthy string of invective, then fixed that one bloodshot eye on me. "And *who* in the name of the Maker sent *you*?" he snapped.

"Me?" I repeated. "No one."

"Then what are you doing here?"

Kyp stepped forward. "We came to find out what all the swearing was about."

He erupted in a flurry of ineffectual flapping and released a stream of additional curses before collapsing back into the muck. Then another thought seemed to strike him and, panting, he struggled to lift his head. "You're not with that mite-ridden, egg-eating Collection then?"

That got our attention. We glanced at one another. "No," Kyp answered.

"Oh," the old bird grunted, and brightened considerably. "Oh, that's different. Well, then. Good eating!"

"And the wind under your wings," Kyp responded formally, although somewhat inappropriately, I thought, considering the situation.

"Well, what are *you* staring at?" he barked at me,

returning to his previous gruff manner. "Haven't you ever seen a Crow who's been in a fight before?"

"Do you want some help?" Kym inquired hesitantly.

"Help? Of course I want *help*," he barked. "You think I want to stay here, stuck in this mess till snakes and snapping turtles pluck me clean? Owl droppings, what do you think I've been shouting about ever since I heard you?"

"What can we do?" Kyp asked.

"You could lift this mink-soiled branch off me. I was fighting down here, and one of these mite-ridden branches sprang from the mite-ridden notch it had been jammed in. It killed those two rascals there and just about snapped my back. I haven't been able to crawl out from under it."

Kyp crouched, crept through the weeds and reeds, seized part of the branch in his beak and pulled. I leaned in, slipped my neck under and pushed up.

"That's it," the old Crow gasped. "Push harder, will you?" He glared up. "You'll have to push harder than that. Although you might want to be a little careful, too," he added as an afterthought. "There may be other branches that will snap back if they're released."

I glanced at Kyp, who just braced his back and pulled harder.

"That's the way!" he growled. "I can feel it giving. A bit more."

The old Crow scrabbled at the mud and flapped his wings. "A bit more," he rasped. Kyp raised his head, his neck muscles straining. I pushed harder, the branch scratching and digging into my shoulders. The old Crow flapped furiously, spattering us with mud — and then suddenly launched himself out from under the trunk.

"There! That's the trick!" he cried triumphantly. "That's the very trick." He lay on the grass, breathing heavily, groaning and stretching his wings. Then he turned his beak to his right leg and scratched it furiously. "Maker of the Maker, I've had an itch I haven't been able to do anything about for days."

It was only then that I saw there was a third dead Crow lying under the branches.

"That's one," he said with evident satisfaction as he eyed the body, "I took care of myself."

He suddenly flapped his wings vigorously, shedding mud and bits of reed stalk in all directions, lifted off the ground, then lowered himself back down. "Well, they still work. You took your time. I've been waiting for one of you hummingbirds to come down this way since I heard you take roost last night."

"We might have come earlier, but," Kym noted, "it didn't sound like you were calling for help, exactly."

"Eh? Oh, I suppose not." He chuckled dryly. "I wasn't sure who you were, was I? But I'd become a little desperate. Trapped under the log. Half drowned. I'd gotten to the point where it didn't matter anymore who you were or what you wanted. I figured I'd either greet you and ask for help or fight you. I didn't want to wait politely in the muck for something with teeth and scales to turn me into scavenge." He peered at me suddenly through his one good eye. "What's that flammery draped around your neck?"

"Humans got careless and I stole it. It's protection," I explained briefly — not exactly a lie, I believe a blow from the owl actually glanced off it — and quickly changed the subject. "How did you get into trouble with these ones?" I asked him, directing a wing at the three bodies.

He settled with some difficulty on a low branch of a nearby bush, then took his time putting his feathers in order. "About a year ago, I flew with a small band of mostly older folk like myself. The Plague fell on us like black flies on an open wound. Terrible time, that. Ruinous. The mite-ridden Plague had its way with us the way a falcon has its way with a sparrow chick. When it was done feeding, I was the only one left standing. I flew solo a short time. Looked to band up with someone over winter. Then along comes this bunch — big Crows, all of them — tell me they're part of this much larger flock. I figure

it's a simple matter of flying together, foraging together, keeping watch for one another — but no,
this one tells me they have *rules*. Oh goodness, yes,
tell you what to do and what not to do, call
themselves the Collection —"

I exchanged glances with Kyp.

"You've heard of them?" the older bird inquired.

"We've come across them."

"Have you?" he asked, and the way he said it made
me think he could guess at what the introduction
must have been like. "Well, I came across them and
then some. Like I was saying, they told me this and
that, some of the most blasphemous frip-frappery, a
mess of weasel waste so complicated I couldn't
follow it even if I wanted to. This one said his
Chooser would be able to explain it better. I said no
thank you very much, I have my own beliefs. They
didn't want to hear that and that's when they sent
those three big fellas to show me which direction the
sun rises. Took me in the air. Oh, they thought they
knew how to take care of me, but I knew a thing or
two myself. Flew down to that log there and wedged
my butt under it. That way I could have a go at them
one at a time, you see? They couldn't come at me
from behind or above. Worked good, too, until one
of the branches jarred loose, cut through the air and
knocked me out. Woke up and I was stuck as a bear
in a badger hole."

"How badly are you hurt?" Kyp inquired.

"This? It's nothing. If I'd had a little more youth and a little less bad back, bad wings and bad eyesight, I might have turned things around. But I'll be ready to fly whenever you give the word."

"You want to fly with us?" I heard that question asked and was shocked at the lack of manners. I was doubly shocked when I realized it was me who had spoken.

He turned to consider me and cocked his head. "I don't want to fly alone, do I? With these cuts and these broken feathers? Might as well call down an owl, lie belly up and offer myself to him."

"You're certainly welcome to join us," Kyp interjected. Which seemed to decide things, because we flew off to meet the others.

"Who Chooses for this bunch anyway?" the oldster asked as we lifted above the treetops.

"Me," Kyp replied.

"You?" The stranger snapped his head about so he could better study Kyp with his good eye. "A bit young to be Choosing, aren't you? And who's this one?" he said, turning to look at me.

"This is Katakata. I'm Kyp."

"Good eating," I said.

He grunted something, which, if you were charitable, might have been "Good eating." Then again, it might have been just a grunt. "What's he?"

he continued. "A yearling? Twoling?" He cast a dubious eye on the rest of the flock. "They all yearlings in this flock? Nothing but yearlings or nearly?"

I squinted at him. "I have six years," I informed him, rather stiffly.

He scrutinized me with his one good eye, then turned to Kyp. "Bit slight for six years, isn't he?" he mumbled. Then he squinted at the glitter around my neck and the magpie who was still flying with us. Took a good look at Erkala and her bright white shoulder markings. He shook his head. "Maker of the Maker, bit of a ripe nest I've landed in all right, I can see that well enough."

I was about to answer something to the effect that we were certainly ripe enough to *save* his mite-ridden carcass from his muddy roost, but Kyp stopped me and asked that I fly backup. As I banked left, I heard Kuru mutter to himself, "Magpies, Crows that aren't Crows, and yearlings performing backup. Maker in the Tree, we better keep our top eye open. We fly into a cloud of really rascally looking midges, it's going to be a fair fight."

CHAPTER 12

And with that, Kuru ru Kykata ru Kolk joined us.

He was older than anyone else in the flock and more badly hurt than we had first thought. He never admitted that he was in pain, but flew slowly, groaned loudly, would glide where he could to save his wings and cursed almost continuously. When we perched or stopped to scavenge, he would gently preen, tug debris from his cuts, tend his wounds and scorch the feathers of the Crows around him with fiery oaths.

He didn't endear himself to anyone. He had distinct opinions about nearly everything, and he offered them freely. He was brusque, profane and curiously devout all at once. Somewhere in the fourth sixth of his third day with us, he flew up alongside Kyp and me and abruptly announced, "Time for prayer."

"What?" I asked.

"Time for prayer," he repeated. "We've flown most of the mucking day. We've eaten. Time for prayer."

"For prayer? Our *Chooser* Chooses that kind of thing. Our Chooser tells us when we will stop and when we won't —"

"It's all right," Kyp interrupted and nodded to a tree we were approaching. "We can stop."

As we took our perches, Erkala dropped next to Kyp. "Why are we stopping?"

"Our honored guest requested it," I said, nodding at Kuru. "Said it was time for prayer."

"He *what?*"

"Look at him," Kyp said quietly, drawing us to a perch some trees over. He nodded at Kuru, draped over a branch, his eyes closed. "He's exhausted."

"If we don't make better use of the wind," Erkala cautioned, "the Collection will be on us."

"We caught a good wind coming down the valley."

Erkala snorted. "Will the Collection stop for prayer? Won't they catch the wind as well?"

"Is it wise to invite an injured to join us when we are making such hurry?" a voice asked. I turned and saw Kymnyt, one of Kym's bunch, perched below. She was a twelve year old who held some considerable respect and weight with those who had been released from confinement among the humans.

It was then I became aware that others of the flock were slowly drawing in closer to hear the conversation.

"The new one," Kymnyt said, flicking her tail at where Kuru was deep in 'prayer.' "He hinders us."

"He's an Elder," Kyp pointed out reasonably. "Every flock benefits from the presence of Elders."

"He carries bad luck to the nest," Kymnyt disagreed and flicked her tail again. I wondered if it was a nervous tick she had developed while in confinement or if she had always had it.

"He and that *other* one — the one who shouts each night," someone said.

"They aren't the only problems. We're tired," objected another Crow farther down the tree. "It's confusing flying as we have."

"There's no peace," Kymnyt continued, "no right-flying." And as others nodded their agreement, I realized she was probably speaking for many in this improvised delegation.

"We don't know the territory. The roost changes every night," another protested. "And now, this new one joins us."

"This is not our way from past times," Kykyru, a comrade of Kymnyt, added. "To travel and travel and travel. When does it stop?"

"Maybe we should speak," Kymnyt suggested, "with these Crows who follow us."

"That's right," several voices echoed.

"What do you mean?" Kyp asked.

"It may be that these who follow us are not even from the Collection," Kymnyt added. "How can we be sure?"

"I *saw* them," Kyrt objected, "with my own eyes."

"But for how long?" Kymnyt asked evenly. "A moment? Not even. You hurried to return with news. Perhaps you were mistaken."

"What about Kyl?" Kyrt asked. "He recognized them."

"Kyl is no longer with us," Kymnyt replied. "The owl took him — may his shade have peace. The Maker only knows what he saw."

"I see," Kyp said, glancing from one face to another. "Kata, what do you think?"

"I'm tired of flying, too. You all know that. No one is more for rest and forage than I. But if Kyp thinks we should keep going, that's what I think as well."

Kyp turned to Erkala. "You?"

"You Choose for this flock," she replied simply. "Why ask?"

It struck me then, how divided we still were. How many of those who were objecting were ones who had been released from the human's roost.

Suddenly a gravelly voice interrupted. "This a council?"

We turned our heads and there was Kuru, still nursing one wing.

"We were just discussing which direction we should fly," Kyp replied. "It's not really a council —"

"Sounds like one. *They're* asking questions," he said, nodding to the delegation. "*You're* answering. Call a loon a jay, it still dives for fish. Don't you think Elders should be invited to council? I'm looking 'round this bunch" — he peered up and down through the branches — "and it appears to me I'm the only one here who fits that description. I have thirty-five years. Anyone here have more?"

No one answered.

"Anyone?" he repeated.

"If you have an opinion, we would welcome hearing it," Kyp invited Kuru, before awkwardly adding the honorific "Uncle."

"Would you?" Kuru said, tipping his head back and looking down his beak at the council. "Would you? Well, maybe I have an opinion. I'm not entirely certain I understand everything I've heard, but I'll tell you what I think. I heard some of you saying that I've slowed the flock down. You know what the Maker told Great Crow. Wings aren't wide enough, legs long enough, fins strong enough. Destiny arrives without introduction and cannot be out-flown. It strikes me that it's not so much speed that's needed now as clear thinking. This talk of holding a conversation with the Collection, of somehow working things out — I don't know when I've heard owl pellets like it. They don't *want* to talk with you. It wasn't *talking* to them that got me this." He turned his head around to display the scar running down his neck. "As for fighting them, well, more owl pellets. This bunch of honey suckers couldn't take those ones I met, and if there're as many as you say there are, you have only one choice. Stay ahead and stay outta sight. And I wouldn't hang about — they told me the rest of them are on their way."

That got everyone's attention. "Of course they're coming. The whole lot of them. Isn't that what they told me? That this Chooser, this Collector, he would be following. Well, it doesn't seem to me that he'd come without his flight mates. Do you think? Of course, I could be wrong. I didn't wait to ask them any questions. And I'd suggest you don't want to wait either."

"We can't be expected to fly every day," Kymnyt protested.

"You *can't?*" Kuru tilted his head back and stared at her coolly. "Why's that?"

"You don't know what conditions we come from, or how far we've flown already," she explained. "We can't just go, go, go every day."

"Why not? You get up when you have to, and you fly when you have to. The day you can't — well, that's the day you become scavenge. The next day you're dust and the wind has scattered you. You think that's too hard? Well, my poor featherless chickling, who told you things should be *easy*? Hey? Who said you could rest when you wanted? What makes you believe that because you had troubles before, there aren't more? Maker in the Nest, you can't even answer the *easiest* questions." Kuru cocked his head and stared intently at Kymnyt. "Do you even know what a tree is?"

Kymnyt looked at him blankly.

"I'm asking you," Kuru demanded.

"What are you talking about?" Kymnyt inquired, confused.

"I'm putting a simple question to you — what's a tree?"

"I don't know what the point —" she sputtered.

"You don't understand my question? Let me ask it another way." Kuru gestured with one wing. "That's a tree over there, yes?"

Kymnyt's tail flicked several times in quick succession. "Yes."

"Well?" Kuru asked impatiently, "What is it?"

"You mean what *kind* of tree?"

"I'm *asking* you, plain as I can," Kuru said, raising his voice, "*what* is a tree? You can answer, can't you?

It's not a difficult question."

"It's a tall, very tall, plant," Kymnyt replied finally. "With branches. And we perch in them."

Kuru laughed bitterly to himself. "Useless," he concluded and shook his head. "Completely useless. Might as well have asked a stone to pick a berry, you're that useless."

And the way he so obviously relished his judgment tickled me, so I may have chuckled. My mistake. Kuru slowly eyed me up and down.

"And *you*?" he barked. "You think that's funny? What about you?"

"What about me?" I asked, bristling.

"Can you tell me what a tree is?"

I tried to ignore him, but Kuru wasn't someone who was easy to ignore.

"Are you going to answer?"

"A *tree*," I snapped, "is a useful, very useful, plant. We nest in it. We sleep in it. What more is there to say?"

"Ha!" he chortled dismissively. "Well, there you go. Useless. All of you, useless. Oh well, never mind, never mind. I've just arrived. You don't have to listen to me. You just *roost*, *rest*, wait for these others in the Collection to arrive, and then you'll be able to *explain* it all to them. I'm sure they'll listen to you. For myself, I've prayed and I hope you've prayed because it looks to me like some of you could use prayer. In any case, I'm ready to fly a little farther if that's what your Chooser wants."

The council that wasn't a council fell apart not long after that, but it was clear which way the wind was blowing. We flew till it was dark, collapsed in a roost and were asleep before we'd folded our wings.

CHAPTER 13

"What?" Kryk woke with a start. The night air was crisp as he opened his eyes. He shook, and dew dropped from his feathers. He was, as usual, perched some distance from the rest of the flock.

A figure approached him out of the dark. The moon glistened on her forehead and shoulders. "You were shouting again," Kym whispered.

"Sorry," Kryk muttered and rose to his talons. "Did I disturb anyone?"

Kym didn't reply immediately, but lowered herself onto the branch as though it was the most normal thing in the world to wake someone and talk to them in the middle of the night. "I was speaking with some of the others," she said at last. "They're concerned. Not just about tonight. They say you have dreams every night."

"Everyone has dreams —" he began.

"They told me," she continued, "that they couldn't understand most of what you said, but that you always called out, 'Stop looking at me.'"

"And I apologize," Kryk said as he glanced about at the other branches. "But you can't control your dreams —"

"What does that mean — 'Stop looking at me'? *Who* should stop looking at you?"

"I don't know," Kryk insisted. "I don't remember."

"And that's partly what concerns the others," Kym explained. "You claim never to remember anything —"

"But I don't."

"— every night."

"And it's not my fault. I'm trying to sleep. I'm trying not to wake anyone. I've tried to keep myself from calling, but it just seems to come out whatever I do, and no one will give me a chance —"

"*Listen* to me, and keep your voice down," Kym continued in a calm, even voice. "I'm *giving* you a chance, right now. No one's heard of your flock or Clan, and we have representatives from many places."

"What's this about?" Kryk protested. "I come from farther away —"

"Stop," Kym interrupted him again. "Don't say anything more. Let me finish. You don't know a thing about flying with other Crows."

"It's just that I haven't flown with anybody in so long —"

"I need," Kym persisted, "to know where you are from —"

"I've told you —"

"— and I want to know how you were caught ... and I want the truth."

Kryk opened and then shut his beak. Kym kept her eyes fixed on him, waiting. He swallowed. "I don't think you do," he said finally.

"Tell me about your dreams."

"I can't," he answered.

"Listen. Please listen to me," Kym said, moving closer on the branch. "There are some in the flock who say that you are too ... ill ... to fly with us. Too unreliable. Too dangerous to us. They have not yet, but they *will* propose that you be Banished. Eventually. If I can't understand what's happening, I won't be able to defend you. Help me to help you."

Kryk shook his head. "Will you believe me, even if I tell the truth?"

"If you tell me the truth, I'll believe you. But it has to be the truth."

Kryk nibbled nervously on the tip of his right wing. He began speaking after a moment, but his voice held a resigned quality. "You asked me where I lived. I lived with humans. I was captured when I wasn't yet a yearling. I have a distant memory of what it was like flying with a flock, but only distant. I never had time to learn anything. I think I may have lived to the south, but … nothing's clear. It wasn't a big flock anyway, maybe fifty. I hurt a wing shortly after I fledged, and while I was on the ground, a human picked me up. Took me away. I was kept inside a human den, in a weave not very different from what you and I and the others were kept in. The humans that lived there would regularly hold me, my entire body enclosed in one of their paws. They slipped something soft over my head that kept light away from me. It — the human — would make the sounds of our folk, calling for help. I didn't know what it wanted from me. But it kept doing the same thing, over and over. Eventually, I called for help, too. And when I did, the human would feed me."

Kym listened carefully. "When you called for help?" she repeated.

"That's right. Only when I called for help. The

human would feed me pieces of meat or fruit every time. Eventually I understood that this was what was wanted from me. It removed the cover from my head and held the food in front of me. If I called for help, it would place the food in my beak." He blinked. "That's not so hard to do, is it? Wouldn't you call for help if you were hungry and someone offered you food?"

He seemed to be waiting for her answer. Kym nodded. "Why not?"

"Of course you would," he agreed, but his gaze appeared to be at something much farther away. "It's what anyone would do."

"So, then what happened?"

"What do you need to know for?" he asked, suddenly irritable. "The human kept me. It fed me. It made me call for help. What more do you want?"

"What happened?" she repeated gently.

He craned his neck as though his head was a separate creature that wanted to flee his skinny body. Finally he carried on.

"When I had learned what it required of me, when I was able to repeat the call whenever it wanted, it took me out of its roost. It would carry me to a grove of trees. It would wrap a vine around my leg, attach the other end of the vine to a tree branch. And then it would point at me."

"Point at you?"

"With its paws. And then I knew what it wanted."

"Which was?"

Kryk closed his eyes. "To call for help."

"And that's all?"

Kryk didn't answer.

"Kryk?" Kym asked again. "Did anyone come?"

He drew in his head and perched silently.

"Did anyone ever come?" she repeated.

"Yes," he replied at last, "almost always."

"Who?"

"Crows. Sometimes only one at a time. Sometimes several. Wondering why I was calling. Wondering what had happened."

"And then what?"

Kryk opened his eyes and leaned his head wearily against the branch. "The human would kill them," he whispered at last.

Kym stared, horrified. "The human would kill them?"

"Yes."

"How often did this happen?"

"Many times. Many, many times. I would call for help. And then it would kill them. Every time." He made a half-hearted attempt to arrange his feathers and settled heavily on the perch. "And after I had done what I was asked to do, I would get fed."

Kym looked at the thin, unkempt Crow, then turned to look out into the night.

"Was it the same humans that kept all of us?"

"No. This was a long time before I was brought to that roost. Once, after calling in some Crows for my human, I developed a sickness. The Plague, I suppose, the same Plague that all the others caught. The human — *my* human — wouldn't touch me after that. The next day, another human came by, placed me in a carrying weave and took me away. That's when I was brought to the roost you found me in."

Kym perched, deep in thought.

"Are you going to tell the others?" Kryk asked.

Kym didn't answer.

"Kym?" he repeated. "Are you going to tell?"

"They have to know."

"If they find out, Kym, they'll send me away. You know they will. No one will want me to stay. No one wants me to stay as it is. But I've changed. I've changed, inside. When I was in the roost, trapped along with the rest of you, I said if I ever get out I'll fly away and I'll live differently. I'll find a flock that doesn't know me or my background and I'll learn how to live like other Crows do —"

"You have to tell them," Kym interrupted him.

"I will, but not yet."

"When?"

"Give me time. You saw that I did something at the human place. I helped to get those fish —"

"You still have to tell them —"

"Let me prove myself. Let them get to know me," he pleaded, "the *new* me. Please."

The night closed around them. Kryk continued staring at Kym.

"You have until Kyp has led us to the Gathering Tree," Kym said at last. "Once we get there, you'll have to tell. Or I will."

CHAPTER 14

The thick fog we'd first encountered along the coast appeared and disappeared as we flew west, and in a way we welcomed it. It was difficult to navigate through, but the fog muffled sound, and of course it also made it difficult to be seen.

After several days of strenuous flying, Kyp stopped to allow us a longer time to scavenge. He had taken a position on the topmost spar of a sycamore and, for all the good it did in that churning murk, was keeping an eye out. There was a sticky stream of sap flowing from a snapped branch on a hickory tree, and Kyf was prying insects up from it, one by one, rolling them over and over against the tree bark to remove the gumminess, and then swallowing them.

I reached past her and carefully lifted a bark beetle. "I could wish for more sun," I lamented as I bit through its crunchy shell, folded it over and swallowed it. "There's a kind of mold that grows on everything in this territory. I believe the tips of my tail feathers are taking on a bit of a green tint."

Her eyes shifted in my direction. "You could stand to preen a little more diligently," she agreed dourly, then rubbed the sap from the tip of her beak.

"She means," Erkala said cuttingly, as she suddenly dropped from a branch above us to another perch, "more than once yearly."

"It's the damp!" I shouted after her and preened furiously. "More than once yearly. There are a lot of things worse than a little mold, and a contrary personality is one of them — she's continually ill tempered, short tempered, cross tempered, sour tempered. It's a very unusual day that you find her without any temper at all," I groused, snapped a tail feather into place and ran my beak across it. "She's spent so much time alone, thinking her sharp, bitter, resentful thoughts, she's barely fit for any company but her own."

"Which makes you two exactly alike," Kyf observed rather unsympathetically and moved over on the branch to inspect another patch of bark for beetles. Seeing nothing there, she lifted her head and looked out through the forest. "I'll take this fog, thank you very much. It's sheltering. Unwelcome guests won't follow what unwelcome eyes can't see, is what I say. And anyway, I enjoy the quiet that comes with the mist — listen to how calm it seems." It was true, only the gentle gurgle of water flowing lazily could be heard, and the distant muffled calling of Crow to Crow.

"Listen to how calm it is?" Kyp repeated suddenly and turned his head to hear better. "And who is it that's calling? Not voices I recognize." He dropped to the branch beside Kyf and quietly told her, "Get everyone out of the tree."

"What?" she asked. "Now?"

"Yes, right now. Listen," Kyp said, turning to Kym, "take everyone you can find to ground, there's fallen timber at the base of the valley. Crowd them all underneath —"

And then I heard another call from a strange throat and saw a distant dark shape cutting through the tree trunks.

"Take your band to ground, under that log," Kyp hissed to Kym, who was perched a branch below. "They'll follow you quickest. Go! Kyf, you take the others down the same way. Kata, Erkala, follow me."

He leaped from the branch. "Split up. Each of you fly separately," he said as we flew. "Go south. We'll gather later by the lightning-struck tree."

"What are we doing?" I asked, confused.

"It must be scouts from the Collection. Call loudly as you fly. Make all the noise you can. We've got to get them to believe the entire flock is moving in that direction. Keep spread out. Attract as many as you can, then once you feel you've got a good number following, slip back." A form loomed close. "Now!" He brought his wings down, surged ahead and began calling as though urging the flock to follow him.

I began calling, too, shouting any old thing, and almost at once heard what seemed like dozens of Crows following me. I closed my beak, slid through a tree, lost those who had been after me and changed direction. A few wing strokes later, I began calling again.

I was startled to hear two new groups of Crows immediately begin to call to one another and give chase. Just east of me, I heard Erkala successfully drawing several other groups off. It was then that I realized we hadn't encountered a scouting band — this was the Collection, *all* of the Collection, and they were everywhere. I changed direction again and began shouting. A shape loomed directly in front of me, I veered right, but it moved at precisely the same time and we almost collided.

"Kyp," I breathed gratefully.

"You weren't supposed to draw them to *me*!" he hissed.

"I didn't mean to," I apologized. "How am I supposed to know where you are in this mess? You didn't tell me the entire Collection would be on my tail!"

"Well, move off *that* way —"

He was interrupted as a stranger separated himself from the fog and came at us.

I immediately went into a tight loop and threw myself at his back. He slipped around me and went straight at Kyp. Kyp spun left as this one attacked, tapped his right wing, and the stranger was brought up hard against a tree trunk, crumpling and disappearing into the billowing fog and dense brush.

"I didn't bring you along to *fight*," Kyp snapped. "I brought you along to *fly*. We can't take them all on, and we can't allow them any excuse to stop and search. Catch their attention. Lead them along the river — the fog lies thickest there. When it's safe, return as quietly as you can. Make sure you're not followed back!"

Away we flew, but now it had become terrifying. The numbers of the Collection weren't immediately visible, but I could hear them well enough. It was hard to hear anything else — their angry voices filled the forest. For a moment, I lost my nerve and was too frightened to open my beak or make even the smallest sound. Then I realized that Kyp was right, if I didn't call, they might inspect this valley more closely and discover everyone.

I sped up and began shouting again. Instantly, what seemed like hundreds of voices responded from every direction. There wasn't time to be scared anymore, I was too busy. Wherever I caught a hint of movement, I quickly shifted right or left. I stayed as close as I could to the ground, so I could maintain some sense of direction, and zigzagged through the underbrush.

In a way, the immense numbers of the Collection milling about worked to my advantage. There was so much noise and confusion that you couldn't hear anything specific for all the racket. In the end, that's probably the only thing that saved me. It wasn't quick thinking on my part.

But there is nothing like fear to put extra wind under your wings. I led those Crows until I felt I had taken them a good distance, then dropped to the ground, panting. Above me, I could hear the roar of the Collection moving steadily upriver, still calling to one another. For a while I heard Erkala's voice, faint and far away. Eventually, when I couldn't hear voices anymore, I slipped back up the ravine.

As it turned out, I returned at about the same time as Kyp. Kyf was perched atop a deadfall that projected out of the river, keeping watch. She called to the others in our flock and slowly they emerged from their hiding spots.

I related how Kyp had dispatched the Crow who had attacked us.

"That was brilliant," Kyf said, bobbing her head with pleasure.

"Well," Kyp allowed, "after this they'll remember that fog can be used to escape as well as to attack."

"That was some very quick thinking," Kym said and leaned a shoulder against him.

"You shouldn't have come," Erkala declared, dropping beside us, her feathers bristling.

Kyp just looked at her.

"You're still damaged," she reproached him, barely suppressing the emotion in her voice. "Your primaries aren't complete yet. Your molt has only just begun. You could have been caught. If others had fallen on you, you could have been taken apart. Then what? Who would have led us? You should have left it to Kata and me, or someone else. It was bad judgment."

She began to say something else, but instead shook her head and flew off.

I watched her go, alarmed at her outburst. "She's just worried about you," I said.

"There's more of them, waa," a strange wheezing voice interrupted. We turned and saw that the magpie that had been tagging along with us since we'd freed her from the human's roost was now accompanied by two others. I realized that although she spoke Crow, I had never held a conversation with her.

"What are you saying?" Kyp asked.

"Waa," she wheezed, "they — other Crows, recent Crows — gather more, many more, waa, since you see them." The magpie nodded off into the trees, where I could see eight other magpies perched. "Waa. My claw and its talons — my" —she searched for the right word in Crow — "waa, band, live this place. This" — she gestured with her beak — "our territory. I speak with them, waa. They look, they count these stranger ones as they pass. You say maybe fifty, waa, maybe sixty different thousands when you see him last?"

"Yes," Kyp replied, trying hard to make out what she was saying past her periodic thrumming. "That's about what there was when we first met them."

"More now, waa —" the magpie wheezed after consulting with her friends. "Maybe, waa. Maybe more by twice. Hundred thousands now."

"One hundred thousand?" I asked. "They're sure?"

She nodded. "Waa. Is strange thing, yes? This many Crow ones, waa, here? My family, waa, they high up, up above fog when Collection ones come. They count as they enter fog. Then they drop, waa, into fog to find out what happens — why so many? — and find me. Now, waa," she thrummed, "now, I leave you, join my blood, waa." She seemed to be nearly finished, but she looked directly at Kyp, and I saw her make an effort to speak Crow as clearly as she could. "But *you*, I remember you, always for what you did. You fetch me out. Out of the human roost. Out of the human weaves. I remember, waa. My blood remembers. Their blood after." She nodded. "Many thanks. The sky sees you and keeps you."

"Good eating," Kyp replied.

The magpie nodded again, then she and the others flew over the rise and away.

"A hundred thousand!" I murmured to myself, "Maker in the Roost."

"With that, I suppose he can afford to send out a few scouts," Kym reflected. She turned to Kyp. "So. Which way do we fly now?"

Kyp looked off into the mist. "I don't know."

"We can't stay here," I pointed out. "When they don't find us up the valley, they'll double back —"

"Not right away, they won't," Kyf objected. "The fog's gotten thicker and it's almost dark."

Kyp nodded, seeming distracted. "Yes. And we have to try to be somewhere else by the time it becomes light again."

"So?" Kym asked gently when Kyp didn't say anything more. "What are you suggesting?"

"Kuper will be expecting us to go west," Kyp began slowly, as though working it through for himself, "and I imagine by daybreak he'll have spread his folks out both north and south. But this weather can work to our advantage."

I failed to see the logic, and apparently wasn't the only one. "How?" Kym asked finally.

"He'll be watching the river valleys and searching the treetops. But in the dead of night, in this kind of weather, he won't want to spread things too thin. Owls will have them."

"But what good is *that* to us?" I asked, still lost. "If we can't see, we can't fly. And we already know too well what owls can do."

"We'll stay close for protection," Kyp said, looking at me. "And we'll start out now — or soon anyway."

"But in the dark —" Kyf said, shaking her head.

"But we won't *be* in the dark," Kyp objected, beginning to sound more confident. "At least, not entirely. Humans have made trouble for us in the past — *now* we'll permit them to help us. We'll follow their moving boxes, and those things make their own light, don't they?"

"But —" I began.

"We'll stay low," Kyp kept on, "and fly behind the boxes. Keep quiet. In this fog and night, as we slip behind the boxes, no one will see or hear us. And if the Collection can't see us, and they can't hear us ..."

"They can't follow us," I concluded.

"That's right. Pass the word through the tree.

Have everyone ready to fly. We'll move once it's completely dark."

The others flew off to ready the flock. I stayed behind. I was still exhausted from the flight from the Collection and wasn't looking forward to an additional flight in the dark.

I shook my head. "We're going to follow the human?"

"That's right," Kyp answered.

"On their trackway? Between all those speeding, swerving moving boxes?"

"Yes."

"And if any of the Collection *is* awake. And *is* set up along the human's trackways, and *does* see us?"

"Well. We'll have a chance to try out Erkala's suggestion," Kyp answered. "Kill them as quickly as we can, before they can warn the others."

CHAPTER 15

We waited and kept watch.

Although we were all concerned about the journey ahead, and nervous that the Collection would return, Kyp insisted that we stay in place until it was completely dark, so that there would be no indication to any prying eyes of the direction we had gone.

During that anxious delay, Uncle Kuru inadvertently managed to attract the attention of wasps when he bobbled a branch they had built their nest on. Luckily, Erkala spotted them swarming and shouted a warning. Everyone escaped without trouble except for the unfortunate Kryk, who for reasons no one could entirely grasp, snapped at one of them and got his tongue stung for his efforts.

It was pretty clear that Kuru's older eyes just hadn't caught what younger eyes had, but far from being ashamed, Kuru found the disturbance the cause of tremendous mirth. Even much later, long after everyone else had tired of it, he would still burst into fits of laughter.

"Snapped at it!" he chortled to himself. "Thought it would make a tasty treat! Great Crow and the First Brood, he thought he would have himself a tender little wasp snack!" Finally Erkala sighed heavily and stirred in one of the upper branches.

"What?" Kuru called up. "Am I disturbing your sleep, Stripes? Interrupting your precious nap?"

Her body stiffened, but she didn't reply. Kuru considered her a moment.

"Here. What about you? Do *you* know what a tree is?"

Erkala leveled a steady gaze at him. "*Why* would I know what a tree is?" she answered archly. "I never have time to perch in one long enough, because certain blind, deaf, old fools are too busy stirring up wasps." And with that she shook herself and flew to the relative peace of another perch.

Kuru watched her go. "Well," he muttered to himself, "she's useless, too, although she's got more backbone than the rest of this limp, lazy bunch of flower pollinators. At least she's a Crow. Although," he grumbled as he settled himself back to sleep, "she's the oddest-looking Crow I ever saw."

In an attempt to keep the peace and at the request of Kyf, Kyp flew to the branch Kuru was perched on. The old bird was rolling an ancient, dried blueberry between his bills, attempting to soften it enough to eat. "Is something bothering you, Uncle?" Kyp asked in a quiet voice.

"*Bothering* me?" Kuru mumbled past the berry. "Why would anything be *bothering* me?"

"You're sure?" Kyp asked. "You're not nervous about flying through the dark? Because we can keep some of the younger ones with better eyesight alongside you."

Kuru snorted. "I don't need *watching* over from this bunch. I've flown longer than anyone in this flock, and I believe I know my way in and out of the tree. Why are you suddenly so concerned?"

"You're the eldest here," Kyp said. "That's a special position in any flock. Others look to you for guidance. And you seem ..."

"Seem *what?*" Kuru snapped.

"Disturbed. Restless."

"Restless?" Kuru repeated and placed the berry on the branch beside him. "Of course I'm restless. I'm always a little twitchy when I fly in a flock that has Chooser trouble."

Kyp glanced out beyond the tree, then back at Kuru. "You think there's Chooser trouble here?"

"Don't *you?*" Kuru responded, staring hard at Kyp. "We don't know where we're going exactly. We don't know how far that Collection is from us. They just about had us for scavenge earlier. Doesn't that sound to you like a mite-ridden choice with mange?"

"So, you object to me Choosing?"

"Object? I wouldn't say I 'object,'" Kuru grumbled. "You're a nice enough young fellow, it seems to me. You've guided your flock this far, and I give you full credit for that, and they certainly seem to worship you. And why? Because you went and traveled a Maker of a long way and freed a bunch of Crows from human confinement. That's all very fine."

"But," Kyp said after a moment, "it doesn't sound fine to *you.*"

Kuru tilted his head back and squinted at Kyp over his long beak. "You really want to know? Fair enough. You went and found this Kym and freed her from the humans. Very good! Does that make you a Chooser?"

"I never said it did," Kyp objected. "The flock chose —"

"Does *flying,*" Kuru interrupted him, "out east to free a Crow make you a Chooser, yes or no?"

133

"No," Kyp replied shortly.

"That's right, no," Kuru said gruffly. "So, what does it take to be a Chooser?"

Kyp thought a moment. "That the flock chooses you."

"Ah," Kuru snorted. "Chooses you. *Chooses* you. Nest of the Nest, a band can choose anyone for any kind of foolish reason. And then that Crow can choose to lead the flock directly into the badger's mouth if he wants, and be nothing but bones and feathers and badger droppings moments later. I suppose I mean to ask what makes a *good* Chooser. What makes that?"

Kyp considered the question. "I don't know."

"That's right, you don't. You're a decent young fellow, good flier, sensible enough by all appearances, but you don't know a lot of things."

"So why don't you educate me? You're the oldest here."

"Me?" Kuru asked, seemingly surprised by the question. "Me? What do I know about being a Chooser? I'm just a cranky Elder with bad eyesight, bad shoulders, feathers falling out all over. If I knew how to be a Chooser, you wouldn't have found me flying solo, would you? I wouldn't have needed assistance from a sorry band like you and your flock of sap suckers and bee eaters." He plucked up the berry again, chewed it a moment longer before finally spitting it out. "Tell me. Why did you go looking for Kym?"

"Because she needed help."

"Is that right?" Kuru asked, squinting again. "Because she needed help?"

"Yes."

"Because *she* needed help," Kuru repeated and edged closer to Kyp. "So you flew *all* that way, took *all* that time, because she needed help?"

"Yes!" Kyp snapped. "I already said yes."

"So it had nothing to do with *you*?" Kuru continued moving even closer to Kyp. "What *you* wanted? Had nothing to do with the fact *you* wanted to see her again?"

"Of course I *wanted* to see her again, I never said —" Kyp objected.

"So what you're *saying*," Kuru continued, over his objections, "is that you flew *all* that distance, and brought *all* those other Crows across water, and into the human colony and into fire and out of fire because *you* wanted to see her again? Is that right?"

"I would have gone *alone*. I *wanted* to go alone. I never asked a single —"

"It doesn't matter who you *asked*. There's hardly anything we get in life because we *asked*. Did you or didn't you do it because you *wanted* to?"

Kyp perched silently a long moment. "Yes," he answered finally.

"Yes. Exactly, yes. So, you did that for *you*. You didn't do it for those sorry Crows who followed you initially. And much good it's done several of them — they're just scavenge for groundlings now. And you think *that's* what it takes to be Chooser? To risk everything and everyone to get what *you* want? A little flying, a little quick thinking, a little risk taking. Hey? Is that what you think? You poor, clueless, innocent chick," Kuru said, suddenly sounding genuinely sad. "We *all* want things, and are trying to get them every day, but that has *nothing* to do with Choosing. Not a thing. And you will be a Chooser, a genuine Chooser, when you do something for the flock that has nothing, and I mean *nothing*, to do with you, or what you want."

Kuru glanced down ruefully at the berry he'd rejected. "There're things you can chew and chew, but they still won't go down easy. I imagine you'll have things to do before we leave this roost. Me, I've got wounds to bathe." And he dropped down to the creek bed.

Kyp remained sitting on the branch for some time on his own, lost in thought. Finally, the bright parallel beams of a red moving box flickered and drew closer. Kyp sounded the signal, and we all shifted to a tree that overhung a nearby trackway. We waited until the box had drawn close, then lifted and fell into place behind it.

At some point, the moving box changed its mind. It uttered a terrible grinding kind of groan and ambled south, but by then another moving box, a dusky blue one, had approached, rattling west. We settled behind this latest moving box and its choking, smoking vapors and followed the yellow sloping beams through the darkness.

CHAPTER 16

And so we began our long flight through darkness. Our plan had been to stick with the moving boxes as closely as possible. This of course would benefit us in several ways. The lights would provide direction and the roar would cover any sounds we might make. As well, having the moving box rumble ahead would clear the track of owls and other nighttime Crow-eating riffraff.

If we flew fast and everything went well, we would be gone before anything — owls, Crows, ghosts or humans — ever sensed we had slipped through their territory. Talking was forbidden, except as necessary. No breaks. No rests. Straight west, always straight west.

The air we flew through was wretched, the dust blown back by the boxes thick and choking. Feathers grew coated over time with an oily sheen. The back of beaks developed a gritty layer of sticky grime.

And it was always dangerous. Apart from the risk of owls, if you didn't pay attention both ahead and behind, another moving box could slide up fast, strike you down and crush you under one of the churning paws. The safest thing was, we discovered, to wait for a relatively slow-moving box, out traveling on its own. Wait till it drew close, then stick with it as it trundled along.

Luckily for us, in the deep middle of the dark six, there weren't many boxes moving along the trackways, and it was easier to find the odd, lone box to attach ourselves to.

Eventually we established a routine. Fly. Find some underbrush to hide in as it grew light. Post sentries. Sleep during the day. Come dusk, move out to the trackways again and find ourselves another moving box to follow.

One night I relieved the crushing boredom of the wretched night flight by gliding up as close as I possibly could and peering into the box ahead. Inside, four humans sat perfectly still, squished one next to the other, their big bulbous heads sticking up like a small patch of fuzzy melons. Kym flew alongside me.

"What do you think they're doing?" I whispered.

"Nothing," she answered. "Humans have an uncanny ability to engage in intense activity — and then do nothing at all for long stretches. It's very confusing."

"When you were confined," I asked, "did they often sit still like that?"

She stared ahead at the resting humans. "Sometimes."

I felt the cool night air billow under my wings and thought back to her period of captivity. "You must hate them," I said.

She shook her head. "No. And I don't think they hate us. But they don't notice us either. Not really. Only when we're in their way."

One of the humans suddenly laid its round, fuzzy head against another's shoulder. It snuggled in and seemed to go to sleep.

"But I mean, are we any better?" Kym continued. "We notice only what we want to notice. We pay attention to the humans only when they have something we need or when they chase us. I didn't even know humans existed until I was a twoling."

I nodded. "As a chick, until I realized not everything was a bird, I thought humans hatched into the world with two bums and no beak," I confessed. "That's how much I knew about them."

Kym chuckled and Kyf flew in close to hiss a testy "Shh." Kym lifted one wing and dropped back.

I continued flying close to the humans. Sometimes — not often, because as Kym said, humans don't pay attention to much of anything but themselves — a human would glance back and see us, dimly outlined against the darkness and dust. It might point and chatter to the other humans crouched next to it. Then the moving boxes would lurch forward, faster than before.

Eventually it dawned on me that, from their perspective, it must have seemed a little as though we were chasing them. When I realized that, I took some small, perverse pleasure in lurching in as closely and quickly as possible. I tried to look especially fierce during these dives and chuckled at the consternation I hoped I was causing.

If it hadn't been dark and cold, and if we all hadn't been bone tired, starved and half-poisoned by their putrid smoke, I might have said I was enjoying myself — until, in the middle of one of my especially threatening charges, Kyp slipped down beside me and asked in an annoyed voice what I thought I was doing.

"Playing a little game," I explained.

"Well, stop it," he said curtly. "Whatever it is they think you're doing, it makes them speed up, and the flock is already flying full out."

At that point I realized how foolish and self-indulgent I had been and felt duly embarrassed.

After that I maintained a more respectful distance.

Without something to distract you, though, it was stressful flying in the dark. Never being able to keep a proper lookout. Not being sure if the Collection was somewhere close behind — or ahead of us. Worrying about noises we heard, or thought we heard. Constantly inhaling fumes and choking on dust.

Just when it seemed that the flock was completely spent and couldn't take another moment under these conditions, Kym approached Kyp and they conferred. They seemed to argue for a short time — I couldn't tell for certain over the din of the moving box — then all at once Kyp signaled to us to follow him.

Abruptly, he dropped back, abandoning the box we had been trailing after, and instead flew directly over an immense, flat, slow-moving box that had been approaching us for some time along the trackway. Without warning, Kyp suddenly folded his wings and dropped to a perch right on top of the moving box. Kym didn't hesitate, but flew down beside him and gestured to me to join her.

I was stunned. It seemed completely deranged, but then, everything we were doing seemed at least a little deranged — and, like everyone else, I was exhausted. So I folded my wings and took a position directly beside Kym.

One after another, the flock joined us and found a perch on the broad back of that enormous, heaving moving box. Soon we were all there, pressed up one against another, perched on the pitching surface, the night air stirring our feathers. If it had been frightening following the moving boxes before, perching on top of one as it hurled itself forward was terrifying and exhilarating all at once. The shuddering, startling power you felt beneath your talons. The sensation of moving without so much as lifting a feather was upsetting and curiously magical all at the same time.

Eventually the moving box groaned and squealed and woke me — I had been so fatigued by anxiety that, impossible as it seems, I'd actually nodded off. It shook, shivered a little and began to turn south. Kyp spread his wings, lifted into the air and called to us. We followed until we found a sheltered roost in a low-standing copse of vine and shrub.

It was nearly daylight. We must have traveled an enormous distance without lifting a wing or stirring a single feather.

CHAPTER *17*

Kyp allowed us to sleep much longer than he normally would have. When we woke, he gathered us together.

"We've managed to stay ahead of the Collection," he began, "but I'm not sure by how much. Kym's notion to catch a ride on one of the moving boxes was inspired — we made good distance, and got some rest as well. But we can't risk doing that often, and some of you have warned me that we can't keep on like this, and you're right. We can't. I thought if we flew fast enough, long enough, the Collection would stop following us. That hasn't happened. I know it's been suggested that we should send someone to talk to them. But when they caught up with us last, they attacked almost immediately." He looked about at the rest of us. "So it doesn't look to me like they're interested in talking. I'm sorry."

No one said anything, until Kyrt asked, "Are you telling us there isn't anything we can do?"

Kyp shook his head. "I didn't say that."

In spite of the sleep, I was still tired and maybe not thinking as clearly as I might. "So," I started, clearing my throat, "what *are* you saying? Have you a plan?"

"The size of their flock gives the Collection a huge advantage. Maybe we can do something about that."

"How?" Kyf asked.

"We can't outfly them. And we can't outfight them," Kyp answered. "Maybe it would be useful to have a larger ally on our side."

As much as I had no particular ideas to add, and wasn't prepared for anything he would have suggested, *that* suggestion took me, and I think all of us, by surprise.

Kyf caught my eye. I shrugged and shook my head. "Like *who?*" she ventured.

"The Urkana," he replied.

There are always a certain number of Crows who chatter quietly in the background during council. All of that stopped. That's the sort of thing that happens when someone suggests visiting a legend.

I was the first to speak again — it seems I'm often the first to speak. I'm not proud of it, but there it is.

"*That's* your plan?" I asked, trying not to express any of the doubt or deep skepticism I felt.

"That's what I've been thinking about these past few days as we flew —"

"Is that — the Urkana — even real?" I blurted before I'd had the opportunity to find a more poised way to express my poorly concealed concerns. "I've heard of it — I think we've all *heard* of it — but I always thought it was —"

"Just a story?" Kyp finished my sentence. "No, I heard of it when I was a chick, and there were older members of the Kinaar who described it."

"Had they *been* there?" Kyf asked.

"I don't know."

"And you don't know anyone who actually has?"

"He has." Kyp nodded up the tree. "He's been there."

All heads turned and we considered Uncle Kuru, who was perched above, wrestling a large spruce cone.

"*Him?*" Kyf exclaimed.

"Yes," Kyp replied.

My eyes slid to Kuru. "*You've* been there?"

He glanced up from his struggle to extract seeds. "That's right."

"*What is it?*" Kyrt broke in. "You say we've all heard of it, but *I* haven't, and I'm not sure that many of my band have. The Urkana is ...?"

"It's an enormous winter flock," I explained. "The way I heard it — when I was considerably younger — was that somewhere in the very center of the flatlands, there's a winter roost where the biggest flock that ever was gathers." I looked over at Kyp. "Urkana means, in the old tongue, 'Where the Wind Chooses,' and I was told that the west wind slept there. I was also told Great Crow founded the flock, and that each night Crows fed from enchanted corn that restored their youth."

Kuru wedged the cone up against the branch, probed between the slats for seeds. "It's real," he declared. "There's no magic corn, and I've been there."

"And it's a big enough group to help us?" I asked.

Kuru plucked up a seed, swallowed it and nodded. "I believe so."

"It would have to be very big to help us against the Collection," Kyf pointed out. "There are how many in this Urkana?"

Kuru shook the cone and then tossed it from the branch. "Over a million. That's what I was told at the time. I was young and didn't do a proper count."

I looked at him. He just stared defiantly back.

"Um. If it's real," Kyrt began hesitantly, "and there are that many, aren't we likely to run into problems of territory?"

"No," Kyp said and shook his head. "It's a winter roost and draws from such a wide area that it has its own rules. Isn't that right?"

"That's right," Kuru answered. "Those who attend abide by the rules, regardless of the flock they come from — even, I'd assume, your Collection. And the numbers are enough that they can enforce their rules."

"We'll be able to get some advice," Kyp pointed out. "Maybe gather support. At the very least we should be able to get some rest."

Kuru fluttered down beside Kyp. "Some call it the Kaa-nyt or Great Crows Cloud because it's that big. From a distance, when you're in the air, that's what it looks like — a great shimmering black cloud." He looked about at the flock. "You think you've seen gatherings, but you haven't seen anything."

"How far is it?" Kyrt asked.

"Well, that's the thing," he said slowly. "I'm not exactly sure. I've been turned around since the Plague, and I haven't visited the Urkana since I was a twoling."

"So," I asked, "you don't know the direction?"

"Not exactly, no."

"Well. If you don't know how to get there," Kyf asked hesitantly, "isn't that as bad as if it didn't exist?"

"I don't think so. We know it can't be far. We've already dropped a good distance south and west," Kyp replied. "The land has been flattening out. The air is drier. We're approaching the flatlands for sure."

"But," I started — I felt the same reluctance to question Kyp that Kyf had, "where do we go from here? North? South? How much farther west?"

"Each night, we have flown after the boxes." Kymnyt, who had been conspicuously silent since her run-in with Kuru, must have felt sufficiently emboldened by the discussion to voice her misgivings. "Flying night by night without knowing a direction. We can't continue this."

Several of those who had been confined sounded their support.

"I think," someone said in a quiet voice, "I have something to add."

We turned and I was surprised to discover that the voice belonged to Kym. Surprised because her voice sounded very unlike her. She had obviously been asleep, and her feathers were still askew. She was perched on one of the lower branches with her head tucked well back into her shoulders, as though she was very cold.

"I was just dreaming," she said, "and it had to do with this Urkana that you were talking about. That is — it wasn't about it, but it was." She stopped and considered the dream a moment. "It was mentioned, anyway."

"Maybe you heard us talking about it," Kyrt suggested, "in your sleep."

"Maybe," Kym answered, sounding doubtful. "I don't think so. But there were several things in the dream that I don't understand, and perhaps you will be able to explain them to me. In the dream there was a storm. It was far away on the edge of the horizon. I could see it, a dark smudge in the west, billowing and growing. The wind was barely stroking the leaves at this point. I turned and glanced in the opposite direction and the weather seemed more pleasant. I thought to myself, Maybe we should go *there*. After all, who wants a difficult flight when one can fly easy? But suddenly this small Crow dropped to the branch across from me. He shook his head. 'This way,' he told me. 'This way.' And he nodded west, in the direction of the storm."

"Kwaku," someone whispered, and a murmur spread through the flock.

"My heart sank," Kym continued, ignoring the whispers, "because even in the short time he'd spoken, the storm had grown. Moved closer. The wind was blowing my feathers back now. The tree was swaying. I shouted to this stranger, over the noise of the wind and leaves, that I didn't want to go that way. He nodded as though he understood, and was even a little sympathetic, but he told me there was no way over, no way around, the only way was to go through it."

She stopped and shuddered, as though she suddenly could feel the effects of the wind she was describing.

"Was that," Kyp asked, "the end of your dream?"

Kym didn't answer at once. She cocked her head to one side and closed her eyes, as though trying to see it again in her mind's eye. "No," she answered finally. "I glanced back again. The storm was even closer. Almost on us. And it was bad, very strong, with bursts of lightning, trees were being bent almost flat, uprooted. I asked the stranger how we could possibly get through this trouble. He flew to the very outmost branch of the tree. 'There's a way,' he said. 'A hard way. A way of tests.' That's the way he said it. 'You can get through this, and you'll learn how at the Urkana,' he said, and he was talking to me as quietly as we are talking now, even though rain was slicing through the leaves and the storm filled the sky, black, heavy, almost solid. 'But before you can be free of this burden and find your way back to the Gathering Tree, day will erupt from beneath you, night will descend from above, the dead will greet you, rocks will fly and the sky will struggle with the earth.'"

"What did this Crow look like in your dream?" Kyf asked in a small voice. "What exactly did he look like?"

"Small. Thin. Unkempt. Feathers sticking up." Kym glanced over at Kyf. "I only met him the once, briefly, so I don't remember him for certain, but it could have been your brother."

The muttering among the flock grew louder.

"But wait," Kym said in a louder voice, "there's more."

"What?" Kyp asked. "Did he provide any other guidance?"

"Not exactly." She sat silent a moment longer and then murmured in a small, worried voice, "He told me," she said, looking directly at Kyp, "he told me that before we could get to the Gathering Tree, you would have to die."

CHAPTER 18

"I think," Kyrt maintained, "that the dream means we *shouldn't* go to this gathering. Shouldn't. Doesn't everything he said mean that going that way is impossible?"

Kyp had released the rest of the flock to forage, but the council stayed and kept arguing.

"Kwaku said it was the *only* way," Kyp reminded him. "And that we would learn what we needed at the Urkana."

"But there were a lot of things in that dream that didn't make sense," I pointed out. "Rocks flying. The dead greeting us. Do any of those seem likely to happen?"

"All that must mean something else, too," Kyp argued, "if we can only figure it out."

"He also said," Kyrt countered, "that you would have to die. And how is that supposed to mean something else?"

Kyp threw his wings open in exasperation. "I don't know for sure —"

"That, at least," Kyrt continued, glancing around at the rest of us for support, "sounds pretty clear."

"I think we have to trust Kwaku and understand that things in dreams don't always mean things as they are in life," Kyp replied. "The storm — well, that means our present troubles, for instance. Rocks flying might mean something else, and when he says I have to die, maybe it just means ... I don't know, maybe it means I have to stop leading the flock. Or maybe it means that an idea I've held on to has got to 'die.'"

"You're wrong," Kyf interrupted in a flat tone. Her attention had been elsewhere, as though asleep or deep in thought, but now she looked up. "You're wrong. Kwaku always said exactly what he meant. He knew before he entered the human's roost that he wouldn't be coming out again. And he means exactly what he's said about you. And for *that* reason I'm against following his advice."

"Kyf —" Kyp tried to interrupt.

Kyf continued overtop of Kyp's objections. "What has his advice got us?"

Kyp moved closer to Kyf, but she backed away. "You know," Kyp said, "that you don't believe that about your —"

"He said the only way out of *these* troubles. Well, aren't *these* troubles ones he helped create in the first place? If we hadn't listened to him, where would we be? I'd still have two brothers, *alive*, for one thing. I can tell you that I wish with all my heart that we had never, ever listened to him. I wish that *he* had ignored those voices, had pretended he never heard those voices. I wish ..." Kyf's voice had been growing steadily louder, and as it did, all other side discussions halted. Now she stopped and took a breath. "I just don't see how we'd be worse off inventing our own troubles, without taking his advice, thank you."

"There are a lot of different ways to interpret a dream," Kyp said tiredly as he tried to draw the discussion to a close, "and most of the things about this dream are impossible for me to understand at the moment. For now, our biggest concern has to be getting free of the Collection. I don't know how close they are, but there are a thousand of them for every one of us. That isn't a prediction. That is a fact. So we have to fly soon. *And* we have to get someplace where we can safely rest. We can't keep on as we have. So, unless someone has a better idea" — he scanned the council — "something we can do right away — for me that means making our way to the Urkana. If we can find it. And if someone comes up with a better plan, we can stop and discuss it. Agreed?"

Nobody said anything. Finally I said, "I suppose I agree."

"And I couldn't agree more," Kuru said. "There's been too much talk already. High time we moved."

"I *dis*agree," Kyf objected.

"I agree," Kyrt conceded. "I just hope we're doing the right thing."

"I agree," Kym allowed, "only because I can't think of anything else."

Erkala said nothing. Kyf shook her head and flew to another bush.

Kyp watched her go and sighed. "Anyone else? No?" No one spoke. "Then the Choice is made."

The rest of us slowly retired to join the others and forage, but Erkala stayed behind. For a time, both Kyp and Erkala preened.

"Chasing something we can't be sure exists," she said at last. "This isn't a plan."

"I've heard the Urkana mentioned in my old flock," Kyp maintained stubbornly, "and Kuru's been there."

She shook her head. "Is anyone less dependable?"

"I have to depend on him," Kyp said. "No one else knows the way. What do you suggest?"

"When I joined you, you told me you had no plan, no sure destination. I accepted that. I accepted we would fly together as long as the wind carried us. There are no regrets. Since my mother died and I was left in this new land," she said, looking off at the others foraging, "there has been only this, you and these others for Family. The magpie thanked you for freeing her. In a way, you freed me as well, and with that comes an obligation."

"There never was any obligation," Kyp began, "and even if there was, you have more than —"

"Let me finish," Erkala continued impatiently. "We all have our own secret and foolish dreams. I hoped to earn a place in this flock, but now, I think that is impossible —"

"There's a place for you," Kyp interrupted. "Erkala, you know there's a place."

"Not the place I wanted," she replied in a brittle, dignified voice. "Not the place I hoped to find."

Kyp opened his beak to speak, but Erkala carried on. "There's no fault. I am not trying to find fault. If we have foolish dreams, we cannot blame the Maker for not granting them. But there is still some service I can do. Some other place I can fill. The Collection is only the Collection because of this Kuper. Without him, the Collection would fracture and scatter. If I were to join them —"

Kyp shook his head. "No."

"Just," Erkala persisted, "long enough to gain his confidence."

Kyp shook his head again. "No."

"I could," she said, looking directly at Kyp, "kill him."

"I don't know that you could," Kyp argued. "He's stronger than you know."

Erkala released a grim chuckle. "I wouldn't put it to a *contest*. I would fall on him when he wasn't looking, even if I only broke a wing —"

"Do you believe the rest of the flock wouldn't suspect? They would never give you the opportunity. Of all of us, apart from me, *you* are the one they are most likely to recollect on sight. They would be on you the instant you approached. When I first met you, you told me that since arriving in this land there were many times you asked the Maker to take you. But you told me then, the Maker demands that we all fly true." He peered at Erkala. "How is this different?"

She met his gaze a moment. "Anyone can choose to leave a flock."

"Are you telling me that you *want* to leave us?" he pressed.

"What I want or don't want may be beside the point," she replied and looked past Kyp. "Six," Erkala continued at last. "If the Urkana is not found within six days, I won't say anything to the others. I will leave, and you will know where I have gone."

CHAPTER 19

The prairie laid itself out in front of us, seemingly without end. All the trackways we followed were level and direct. Sometimes the humans had planted slender glowing devices in the dry, brown soil along their trackways, and we would fly by their dim glow. Sometimes for long stretches we would trail one of the human's moving boxes, flying silently over its head, following its glimmering embers, as though it were a star sent to Earth to guide us.

After four days, we hadn't seen any other Crows, or any Urkana either. Kyp allowed us to rest through the dark six — and it was very welcome. Traveling at night had created anxiety in all of us.

We crouched within the close cover of some low-hanging bramble and thorn throughout the day, unable to truly relax, feeling cramped, restless and edgy. Eventually we drifted into a fitful sleep. Around the second sixth we received a surprise guest.

A shaggy, heavy brown-and-black striped cat padded through the brush, head down. It wasn't really aware of what it had entered, when suddenly, just as it was about to trip over her, it *saw* Kyf — really saw her — on the ground.

And then I woke up. I woke up and realized it wasn't a dream I was having — or at least I was only partially dreaming. And it was me who was supposed to be on watch as the others slept. I stood and stepped forward and at the sound of my standing, Kyp woke and rose hurriedly to his talons on the other side. This was followed by Kyrt and Kym jumping up. And with each awakening of a new Crow, you could see a portion of that cat's smug confidence drain away. Finally, Erkala rose right beside him, her feathers rigid, her neck thrust forward, and that was more than enough. That cat released a querulous, disappointed meowl and scampered *backward* faster than any cat has ever run forward — leaving only delicate traces of brown and black fur on the brambles to let us know that it had actually been there.

I was startled, I admit I was startled. And humiliated. How I drifted off when I should have been keeping careful watch, I don't know, except that we were all tired beyond tired.

It probably would have meant nothing at all, except that when I turned around, I found Uncle Kuru staring directly at me. Then he shook his head and began chuckling to himself.

"Nest of the Nest," he chortled quietly. "Nest of the sacred Nest, your watch was a bit of a *sorry* mess, wasn't it? Caught with your head under a wing, hey?"

I was exhausted and, as I said, startled, and before I thought about it, I found myself snapping, "Not so far under a wing as yours was the day the Collection found *you*, I guess."

Uncle Kuru stopped chuckling. He cocked his head to one side, squinted and said, "And three Crows ended up on the ground for their efforts. How many cats did *you* lay flat today, chickadee?"

"Well," I snorted, "'three Crows ended up on the ground for their efforts' is the way *you've* told that story, anyway."

"And what," Kuru said, slowly bristling, "do you mean by that?"

"Well, maybe you were setting up to fight those three from the Collection, and maybe you were just flying away as fast as you could. Maybe that branch sprang out and you got lucky."

Kuru sucked air in and released it slowly. "It's a sad, small individual who blames others when he's at fault himself. I know what I know, you can be certain of that."

"Absolutely. And you're sure of *everything*, aren't you? Everything except the things that count most."

"And what is *that* supposed to mean?"

"How many days' flight is the Urkana from here?"

"I can't say for sure, can I? I've already told you I haven't taken this route before."

I stepped closer to the old Crow. "So is it a *day's* flight from here?"

"I don't know!"

"Or is it two days?" I demanded and moved another step closer. "Three? Twelve? Fifteen? Or are we just plain going in the wrong direction?"

Uncle Kuru's squint squeezed so tight it was as though his eyes shut completely, except for a tiny, dangerous glittering crumb at dead center.

"You're a storyteller, that right?" he asked at last, his voice taut.

"I tell stories," I allowed.

"Why don't you tell a story, then? Do you think that's what this flock needs right now — more questions? What a ripe nest and exposed perch." He made a show of preening, then folded his wings and muttered, "Don't even know what a tree is."

"A *tree*?" I shouted, louder than I'd intended. "I'll tell you what a *tree* is, *Uncle*. A tree is a plant. A plant with branches and a lot of leaves. We roost in them. That's all! *Everyone* knows what a tree is except for the odd, old blowhard who wants to make himself seem more important by turning it into some kind of mystery. A mystery that would make him appear more knowledgeable, more important and more mysterious than he actually is, and keep others from realizing that he has absolutely *nothing* to say."

We perched there with other Crows looking at us, wondering what we'd do now. Kuru didn't make any kind of move. Just continued to size me up. Then suddenly he glanced around at the others and began talking in the mildest way, as though nothing had passed between us.

"I'll give you a story then, since our storyteller doesn't seem inclined. Maker looked out one day over Earth and decided to visit. Didn't come as herself. Came as someone else — the Maker can do that, you know how it is. This time she came as a broad-winged, long-necked vulture. Those ones soar high and see everything. She met a Crow in her first little while out and was happy for it. 'Good eating,' she greeted him.

"Well, this Crow wasn't shy. He set to bragging right away. 'I've been everywhere,' he boasted, 'and I've done everything. I'm so smart I know whatever there is to know.'

"Maker was a little taken aback by this kind of talk. Looked this Crow over, and said, 'Is that so?'

"'That's so,' replied the bird shamelessly. 'The names of the creatures and all their roosts. The parents of all the greater and lesser winds. Where stars go when day breaks. What lies deep beneath the earth and below the swelling seas.'

"The Maker eyed him. 'I might know something you don't,' she suggested in a quiet voice.

"The smart bird just shook his head, said, 'I don't think so.'

"Maker said, 'Maybe we should put it to a test.'

"That Crow wasn't listening, didn't hear the threat underneath. He just puffed out his chest feathers. 'If you knew just how much I know, you wouldn't make your claim,' he said. 'But no, no, I won't compete with something as large as you. You might become offended when you lose and then where would I be?'

"So the Maker made herself smaller, became a sparrow hawk. Now, by this change alone, that Crow should have realized he wasn't dealing with something normal, but he just couldn't humble himself. 'That's smaller,' says he, 'but it's still bigger than me.'

"Maker says, 'Fine,' and she smalls herself down to the size of a flea."

Kuru cocked his head and glanced sideways in my direction. "You know what a flea is, I hope? They're teeny insects just this big, hardly larger than a speck of dust —"

"I *know* what a flea is!" I snapped, his taunting getting under my skin despite my efforts.

"That's all right then, I just didn't want to *confuse* anyone. Didn't want to make a *mystery* of anything. So, where was I? Oh yes, she turned herself into a flea, and that Crow, you know what that Crow did, smart as he was? Clever as he was? He fires off his first question right away. 'What's dark as a cave, deep as a pit, has a way in, but no way out?' And before the Maker could properly reply, he leaned down low, opened the dark entrance to his beak and, with a snip and a snap, he *swallowed* the Maker! Swallowed the Maker, flea head and body, and teeny-weeny flea legs and all — and provided the answer to his riddle at the same time!

"So the Maker's on the inside and that smart Crow is on the outside, and he feels pretty big now — and pretty smart too. That is, until the Maker turns herself into a brood of wasp larvae and they latch on to that Crow and eat their way out. Takes them a little while, but by the time they're finished, there's nothing left of Smart Crow but bones for the wind to whistle through."

And Kuru turns to face me. "You know that story, Storyteller?"

"I've heard something like it before," I replied.

"Is that right?" Kuru asked. "Well, I'm sorry then, if it was all a repetition for you, but I guess the point is at least I'm Crow enough to say that I don't know everything, *and*," he added, flying off to a higher perch, "at least I know better than to swallow something that's bigger than me."

I was about to answer back something unpleasant when a shout interrupted us. I threw up my wings and went to see what it was all about. I was surprised to find that Kyp had perched high on an old, gnarled willow, and was making all the noise.

"What is it?" I called as I approached.

"Come look."

I landed heavily on his perch and glanced about as the branch wobbled to a standstill. I couldn't see anything that would cause alarm. Kyp nodded.

"There" was all he said.

On the very farthest edge of the western horizon was a windswept stand of trees, and just above them, a rising and falling cloud.

"What *is* that?" I asked, squinting.

"That, storyteller," Kuru said, flying up beside me, "is the Urkana."

And this ... this is where I must stop, Cousins. This portion of the story requires more of me than I have right now. There are those of you who will have grown hungry and those of you who need water. I certainly need a drink and a stretch and a chance to catch my breath.

Part Three

CHAPTER 20

Gather in and perch close, Cousins. Find your place on the branch.

The most formal beginning of Great Crow's Recovery of the Sun starts in this fashion:

"Into the night, and out of the night.
A bitter roosting, a tiring flight."

It's a fitting way to begin this portion of our story as well.

Sit closer, my Cousins, sit closer, and listen.

"Uncle, you will accompany me?" Kyp asked.

Activity had swept through the tree as Kyp called the flock up to view the Urkana. We quickly discussed the best protocol for introduction. Kuru had advice about how to approach — but then, when didn't he have advice? — and we all knew that he hadn't attended in some long while. Nobody could say for certain if his advice was still current. What if there was a question of territory? What if things had changed and the scout was attacked?

Kym perched beside Kyp. "Should it be you who goes?" she asked. "You've been standing watch. You're tired. It might be worth sending another speaker in your place. It's not always the Chooser who has to go."

Kyp seemed completely unworried, however. It was as though, having finally encountered the Urkana, all his concerns had disappeared. He simply answered, "Oh, I think I know how to fly there," and then hastily rearranged his feathers.

Kuru was, of course, selected to accompany Kyp, and if Kyp looked almost eager to begin, Kuru — for the first time I had ever seen — seemed to seriously weigh the responsibility of the situation. In that moment, I think he may have begun to wonder how much things might have changed since he last visited the Urkana.

The flock elected that I should go along as well, to provide some kind of protection. I was grateful to be given the opportunity to redeem myself after my failed watch. Once sentries had been posted and Kyp had had a few words with Kym about what the flock should do if he encountered any difficulty, Kyp turned to Kuru and called, "Uncle? Are you ready?"

Kuru nodded twice. Once in answer to Kyp, and once, I believe, as encouragement to himself. "Yes," he replied a little more loudly than he had to. Then he slipped off the branch and we were away.

Kuru chose the direct route. In broad, easy strokes he and I crossed the field, heading for a tree that was set off a little from the rest of the grove. Kyp, however, elected to put on a bit of a display instead.

There is no Crow alive that is not impressed by ability and agility in flight. Kyp demonstrated both. He stalled, swooped, performed dives that took him within a feather's width of the ground. He rolled, climbed, did everything but turn himself inside out. Even some in our own flock had their eyes opened.

Uncle Kuru remained on his perch, waiting patiently, but when Kyp came to perch next to him, he leaned in his direction and whispered, "You've just impressed the Elders of the Urkana and made fans of the youngsters. Very clever."

I scanned the sky, but the Urkana seemed not to have noticed our arrival.

"What now?" I asked.

"We wait," Kuru answered patiently. "They've seen us. They'll send a delegate in good time. They're in no hurry."

Kuru set to grooming, as did Kyp. I glanced about at the empty, open landscape. A single slender human trackway crept across the prairie, but beyond that, nothing marred the simple, pure lines of sky and earth.

"This is a good place," I commented. "They're right when they say the wind Chooses here."

Kyp faced into the wind, the force of the breeze pressing his feathers flat. "That's what I was thinking, too. Can you taste them?"

"What?" I asked.

"The different flavors?" He inhaled deeply. "The air is so rich, you could feed off it."

Suddenly a branch dipped on one of the distant trees. A large and ancient Crow slowly curled high into the air. Two younger Crows rose beside him, and together they made their way to where we were perched.

"Good eating," Kyp greeted them as they landed.

"Good eating," the Elder replied and tipped his head at Kyp and me, "and may the Maker lift and guide you to a safe roost. What brings you cousins to the Urkana?"

"The wind," Kuru replied.

"The wind guides everything," the Elder agreed calmly. "And how long will you stay?"

"Until the wind changes," Kuru answered.

"Good eating, good eating," the Crow murmured, instantly becoming more relaxed. He nodded to the two others who had accompanied him, and they rose into the air and returned to the Urkana. "I see you've been here before and know the responses."

"Not me," Kyp said, shaking his head, "but my Uncle has."

"Ahhh." And the Elder turned his attention to Kuru. "*You*," he said after a particularly penetrating scrutiny, "have the look of someone I might have met back when these trees cast smaller shadows."

"A lifetime ago I perched in those branches for a short period."

"Then perhaps I *do* recognize you. There aren't many Crows our age anymore. We'll have to perch and talk once you're settled in. And you Choose for this group?"

Kuru shook his head. "No, this one here, Kyp ru Kurea ru Kinaar, Chooses."

"Kinaar?" the Elder mused. "Then you're from a considerable distance to the north. But your approach is from the east."

"There are many stories we have to tell," Kyp replied.

"And many days for us to listen to them. I saw your approach," the Elder said, peering directly at Kyp. "You fly as Great Crow must have when he wished to celebrate."

"It was only the flight of the greenest newling," Kyp answered modestly.

"A newling?" the Crow repeated, chuckling to himself softly. "A newling. Maker's Blood, I hope *all* our newlings will fly this way in the future. You, at least," he continued, nodding at Kuru, "have been here before, so I don't have to tell you everything. I am Ur-Kwyt ru Katu ru Kwyt, eldest of my Family. I presume that you know the law. Permission is needed to enter — and you have it. And permission is required before you leave. The Urkana meets over the winter season, and during that time, a single voice must speak for all the separate groups that choose to roost together in this nest. Otherwise there would be chaos. There are how many in your band?"

"Just over a hundred and fifty."

"Among those four trees back there," he said, gesturing with a wing, "are nearly six hundred thousand Crows. You understand? And there is only one voice that speaks here, the council that represents the voice of the Urkana." He paused and closely considered the three of us. "This law while you are here. These rules while you are here. You agree?"

"Of course," Kyp answered.

"Then bring your band to roost. They look tired." And he dropped from the branch and promptly flew off.

"Well," Kyp said, heaving a sigh of relief as the Elder slowly retreated across the field, "we did it."

"Yes, we did," Kuru said and sighed as well. "Yes, we did. And good eating to all of us for making it happen. It's something for an older individual like myself to return to this particular roost. You two chicklings wouldn't understand. There are memories of mine nested in those trees. It's been a long time," he said, "and a long, devious, complicated journey it's been." He turned and squinted at Kyp. "Thank you. It was some flight you took us on."

Kyp shrugged. "And thank *you* for guiding us straight."

"There were times when I wondered if I was, and I'm fairly certain I wasn't the only one," he said, glancing sidelong at me, "who had doubts. Anyway," he added, unfurling his wings, "we'd best let these others know they can fly ahead. They'll be getting nervous."

CHAPTER 21

Something new happened to Kuru the moment the Urkana was sighted. Arriving in that place, among all those other Crows, altered his character in some mysterious and welcome kind of way. It was as though he suddenly became — not young exactly — but younger. More confident. Calmer. Everyone remarked that he cursed less — though when he did curse it was with the same energy and invention as always. And while the change was most drastic in him, it was possible to see signs of something similar in almost every individual in our flock. The anxiety that had been our companion for so long found some other place to perch.

We found a roost in a tree near the others and made ourselves comfortable. It was strange, after flying so long on our own, and so quietly, to hear the constant chatter and clatter of other Crows. Six hundred thousand Crows take up a lot of space, and there were simply Crows *everywhere*. In the trees. Chasing one another above the trees. Stalking through the grass beyond the trees. Grooming one another. Departing to find food, or returning to report having found it.

That first day almost everyone in our flock spent in rest, enjoying the sun and feeling the air stroke our feathers. For the first time in what seemed a lifetime, we had nowhere to go. Occasionally someone would announce they had found scavenge, and those who were interested would fly off to inspect. I and about sixty others flew to an immense field of corn and prowled among the broken stalks. There we found borer worms and larvae of all sorts, the odd dried cob to nibble on, and mice and voles as well. We ate heartily, and it was interesting how secure it felt to eat in the company of all those others.

Even Kyf, who had been largely silent since we'd arrived, seemed to take comfort in organizing us in our new roost.

Just before the second night set, I perched on a sturdy branch that held subtle signs of Crow wear and tear over the ages. Little nubs that had been smoothed, worried and worn until almost every bend or crook seemed especially crafted for the comfort of Crows.

The sun gave one last golden wink over the rim of the horizon and slowly spread its orange and red feathers across the entire western sky. Kyp perched next to me, whetting his beak against a branch. "*You* look happy," he reflected as he vigorously rubbed his beak back and forth across the bark.

"I am. Listen," I urged him.

"To what?" He tilted his head to one side.

"Stories, my friend. Hear them?" We both stopped what we were doing. The chatter of six hundred thousand Crows filtered to us through the hushed shiver of leaves and the gentle hiss of the wind. "Many, many stories."

Kyp took in all the Crows perched around us and all the Crows scattered near the base of the trees. "There's plenty of talk being passed from branch to branch, that's true," he allowed.

I shook myself. "How long? For how many hundreds of generations have Crows gathered here? What would it be like to know everything these old trees know?"

"It would be something," Kyp agreed drowsily, more happy for me, I think, than really intrigued by the stories or the trees or anything else. "Something that you, my friend, will have to ..." He trailed off. To my surprise, he had settled into a sound, deep sleep.

Darkness descended. The tree rocked gently as the breezes sang to us of their travels. I heard only the very beginnings of those songs before I too was asleep.

CHAPTER 22

The air, when I woke, was still and cool.

The sky swept overhead, a perfect deep blue
dome. The day seemed prepared to warm once the
surface mist burned off. I stretched and rearranged
my feathers. When I'd had time to gather my
thoughts, I noticed that Kym had perched herself
three branches up and was facing into the first
flaring of the rising sun. I flew up to join her. "Good
eating," I greeted her, but could tell she was
preoccupied with thoughts of something else.
"What is it?" I asked.

"Look," she said, nodding east.

I turned my head and squinted. Swinging over
the horizon, a dark smudge appeared to hover just

south of the dawning sun — flying level with the ground and growing closer. The Collection, I realized. Suddenly, they halted. For a moment there seemed to be some confusion among the flock. They cast about north, circled back, then selected a distant grove of trees and descended.

We continued watching them, but they didn't send any Crows forward to receive permission to enter. I glanced over as Kyp fluttered to a branch and joined us. "What's he going to do?" I asked.

Kyp rubbed his head against a branch. "I don't think he knows."

Kyrt hopped up from one of the lower branches, and Erkala and Kyf flew down at the same time.

"You saw?" Kyf asked.

I nodded.

"What's he waiting for?" Kyf asked. "Why doesn't he approach?"

Kyp nibbled thoughtfully on a cone. "Well. Life has just gotten very complicated for Kuper. Part of him sees this as an opportunity to recruit. Part of him must know how close he came to catching us, and he's eager to finish things. But once you've stirred the anthill, you can't force the ants back into the nest."

Kyf squinted. "It's still early. You're going to have to be clearer than that."

I answered for him. "Kuper can't graciously invite everyone to join him in his mission and at the same time let them know he tried to kill us because we wouldn't — that's likely to put a burr under the feathers of some of the Elders here."

"That's right," Kyp agreed. "And he doesn't know how long we've been here either, or what we've been doing. He doesn't know what we've said or what kind of understanding we have with the Urkana."

"So, by getting here first you've managed to put him off balance!" Kyrt exclaimed.

"A little," Kyp allowed. "The situation he'll be entering is a bit delicate."

And for the first time I saw a new side of Kyp. Or maybe it was a part of him that had developed sometime during our journey. I'd always known he was smart, but there was a subtle part of him, a part that was somehow able to peer into the future, turn things over in his mind and test them.

"I knew you were up to something!" Kyrt blurted. "I *knew*, when we were flying back there behind the humans, I kept thinking that you must have a plan. I knew it!" he finished happily and flew off to share his discovery with some of the other youngsters.

We watched him perch and talk excitedly with others. "That one," Kuru said, shaking his head, "could stand to worship you just a little less."

"Well, it's not such a bad thing if he feels good now. We'll have to convince the Crows here that Kuper's wrong. And," Kyp added before flying off, "there's still the small matter of us getting clear of the Collection."

CHAPTER 23

Next day the Collection gathered its delegation and sent it out to gain permission to approach. Kuper and two others — the two scouts Kyp had injured back when he directed them to take his message — made up its party. Throughout the Urkana, activity had been taking place for some time as Crows rose from the tree to take a better look at the approaching strang-ers and then dropped back to the branch to discuss things with their relatives.

Word was that the Urkana had never in its entire history seen a single flock of this size approach. Elders in the tree wondered aloud if it didn't portend something special. Within our own tiny flock there was a good deal of heated discussion about how best to deal with their arrival.

"Shouldn't we tell the Urkana what the Collection has been doing?" Kyrt asked.

"We have to tell them," Kyf agreed.

Kyp looked skeptical. "What exactly would we say?" he asked. "That the Collection invited us to join them?"

"That they *chased* us all the way from the ocean," Kyf replied. "That we only just managed to escape them. That they tried to *kill* us."

Kuru shook his head. "I have to agree with Kyp. In a way, what the Collection has done beyond these trees will have *nothing* to do with the Urkana or what they decide," he warned. "Crows gather here, representing many Clans and flocks and Families. There are often conflicts that they have, but the only abiding rule that guides the roost is that those who perch must obey the rules of the Urkana. What happened between us and the Collection before we arrived will mean nothing to anyone. It will simply look like a struggle over territory. And — something else to consider — the Urkana tends to admire strength. You all saw how impressed they were with Kyp's demonstration of flight. How will it look to them if we tell them we fled? Let's wait and see how the Collection handles things and develop our strategy from that. I'd venture that they won't say a word about us."

Kyf snorted. "What could they say about us?"

"Whatever the Collection has to say," Kym observed, "I can't imagine that, if Kuper is speaking for them, they will be able to *persuade* anyone of anything. I knew him as well as anyone did, other than Kyp, back when he was part of the Kinaar. He kept to himself and was a terrible speaker. I honestly can't see how he will convince anyone of anything."

CHAPTER 24

The arrival of the Collection, when they finally negotiated their entrance, was impressive. After receiving permission, they lifted and flew silently in a long, sky-darkening cloud that passed over and above us for some time. Finally they settled in several trees at the far end of the grove. As they perched, I could sense the anxiety ripple through our much smaller group.

Kuper wasted no time. Shortly after he'd arrived, word was passed along that he had asked to speak to the Urkana, and a special assembly was convened just before sunset.

The sky slowly grew purple and orange, as branch upon branch of Crows gathered. The Collection assembled primarily on the northern side of the grove, but there were a number who perched in a tree adjoining ours on the southeast side. A human trackway edged behind a line of older oaks, but the moving boxes roared up and down it only rarely after sunset, so many of the Urkana found perches among these trees. The west side of the grove was free of trees and looked out over open prairie. Kuper found himself a place on a branch of a low, sprawling bush situated near the center of this glade.

Ur-Kwyt introduced him to the flock, welcomed him and then left him alone to speak.

"I woke one morning," Kuper began slowly, his head down as though recalling some distant memory. "The Maker was speaking to me. It wasn't with *words*. And when I say I woke up, I wasn't asleep in the way we normally think of sleep. Not the way you are when you're asleep in a tree. I was asleep and flying, asleep and eating, asleep and speaking. Asleep and awake, Cousins. But still the Maker woke me."

He stopped, and for a moment I wasn't sure that he was going to continue. He seemed deep in his recollection. "She woke me," he began again, finally, "and since then I haven't been able to return to sleep. She's speaking to you, too. She's trying to wake you."

I remarked then just how harsh and grating his voice was and — as Kym had suggested — how un- natural it was for him to be selected to Choose, how ill-suited he was to leading, in many ways. But his conviction was so complete and sincere that, despite his lack of speaking skills, it was hard not to be drawn in by what he said. Throughout the Urkana, through every tree and branch, I could see that every Crow listened attentively.

"I'm not a talker," he explained. "I didn't want to say anything to anyone. I don't normally have much to say. But the Maker ... the Maker didn't care what I *wanted*. She said 'Go and collect my flock.' 'Collect them for what?' I asked her. Collect them to die of the Plague? Collect them so that we can struggle through the winter only to perish in the spring? Collect them so we can be chased from roost to roost by the human?

"'Collect them,' she told me, 'to restore them to their proper place. Collect them so they can survive these bad times.' Because these *are* bad times, Cousins, you have to agree. Who here has not had someone close die in this Plague? Who here has not seen someone killed by the human? Poisoned by the human? Stung by the human? Had their nests knocked down by the human? And our response has always been to fly, to migrate, to retreat, to find our own private places where we can hide, pray, purify, rest and wait for the next opportunity to be chased and harassed."

Here Kuper leaned back and took in the entire flock. "But the Maker has a new message. She told me if you have no fear, nothing bad can touch you. And she tested me, Cousins. She tested me." His voice faltered a moment, as though he had to search out some additional strength or resolve.

"Some of you," he began once again, "already know that the human captured me. Held me. Kept me confined. It was the worst time of my life. I didn't think I would survive it. When I was in confinement, I believed it was punishment, but I later realized that the Maker allowed that. The Maker *wanted* me to know what that felt like. She *wanted* me to know that she could put me in the worst possible situation, place me in the human's power — then release me as easily as a dandelion seed is released from the husk.

"One day, when the time was right, the Maker whispered to me, 'Go.' The human reached to hold me, and I bit it. And with that single bite, I distracted the human, and I leaped out of its reach. And I escaped and flew away. Free."

"Do you see? The Maker has allowed the Plague to pass us by. She has given us a special gift. She is saying it is *time*, Cousins. Time for us to leap out of reach. Time for us to collect, to gather together. Time to change. She is telling us not to fly, but to take. Do the humans have food? Take it. Do they cut down trees where we would roost? Use theirs. We, the Collection, have raided — without caution, without restraint, without *worry* — from the humans wherever we go, and there is always good eating. Look at us, Cousins. There's not a skinny Crow to be found among the Collection. We have enjoyed good eating wherever we went."

Suddenly Kuper leaned forward. "Was this world," he called, "created for the human?"

Members of the Collection shouted "No!" in response.

"That's right. Aren't we told that we were created first? That we flew with the Maker? Alongside the Maker? Wing by wing with her? And now we skulk in the shadows. Perch fitfully. Scavenge cautiously. Well, Cousins, I would *rather* die. I would rather be plucked from the roost. I'd rather be done with this life than live my meager existence praying and purifying and hoping that the human won't snatch anything more from me. That it will leave me *something*. That the human will at least leave me my dignity. Above all, Cousins, the Maker has told me No More."

His flock roared, "No More."

"No more," Kuper repeated and nodded his head. "No more. That's right. The Maker told us to Collect. And we are that Collection. We invite all others to join us. We go where we will, even into the human's perch if necessary, to get what we need. So — how much caution will we show?"

"None!" his flock answered.

"Will we *fly* from the human?"

"No!"

"*Retreat* from the human?"

"*No!*" the Collection shouted again, and the intensity and exhilaration of their response was so strong it took a conscious effort not to join in. I noticed that many of the Urkana were shouting as well.

"Will we hide?" Kuper asked.

"No!"

"Will we take back our land? Our nests? Our roosts? Our lives?"

"Yes!"

"And if we can't," he continued, lowering his voice, "if the human's Plague, its stingers, its poison, its traps, prove too much — then what?"

"We die," they chanted.

"And where will we go?"

"To the Maker."

"Where?"

"To the *Maker!*"

"That's right. To the Maker." He shook his head, as though the ritual had released him of any tension or anxiety or concern that he had ever had. A breeze ruffled his feathers. He lifted his head, flapped his wings and laughed aloud. "Cousins, we *make* things difficult — but truthfully they aren't. Everything is so simple. Why should we fear? We know who we are. We know where we're going. We know the Maker has a perch set aside for us at her roost.

"Urkana in the old tongue means 'Where the Wind Chooses.' The wind blew us here, Cousins, and it's the same wind that is urging you on. Join us, brothers, sisters, join us. Good eating, Fair flying, the Maker's blessing and no more fear ever." His gaze took in the assembly. "I have nothing else to say."

I looked around at the immense flock, spread out among the trees — still calling. Still chanting, still caught up in his message. You could feel the excitement and energy rippling through them.

I turned to Kym, leaned in close. "You're right," I said. "He seems very reserved."

CHAPTER 25

"Well?" I demanded. "What should we do?"

The Urkana had called an end to the discussion and agreed to allow everyone to return to the roost, to think. We had spent our time trying to consider our options.

"That speech of Kuper's has dropped mites in the nest," I observed. "I thought he might speak directly about us. I felt he would probably invite a few from the flock to join him. I never imagined he would have the nerve to issue a general invitation to the entire Urkana. And if he did, I never dreamed that the Urkana would receive it like this. Now, we can't leave without asking permission first. And if we were to leave, there is nothing to stop the Collection from following us — with potentially many more members than they had before."

"All true," Kuru agreed, nodding, "but the good thing is that while we're here, everyone must abide by the Urkana's rules. And that means that at the very least, the Collection will have to be patient. The traditions of this roost stretch into the distant past, and it's the Elders here who have the say. Nothing will be hurried, and nothing would upset them more than if that Kuper were to break their rules."

"But do you think he'll actually convince them to join?" Kyrt asked.

"You heard. He was very persuasive. We speak tomorrow, and we'll have to say something that will change minds."

Kyp remained at the edge of one of the outer branches, staring pensively at the prairie. "Kyp?" Kym asked. "You haven't offered an opinion."

"I'm not the one to ask," he answered without turning about.

"What do you mean?"

"I mean I got it all wrong, didn't I?" he replied bitterly. "I came here hoping to find help. I never really thought anyone else would seriously listen to Kuper. But ... if the Urkana listens to him. If they listen, if they decide their mission is to ... punish the human, how long can it be before the human responds? And who knows then how bad things will get? And I brought all that here, to these Crows. That's what my *plans* have resulted in." He looked up at us, completely miserable.

"Kyp," Kym began.

Kyp shrugged her off. "I have to think," he said, and flew off.

"Should someone follow him?" Kyrt asked.

"And do what?" Kuru asked. "He's right. Sometimes there's no way out of the badger's den but through the badger's mouth. Tomorrow he'll have to say his piece. In the meantime, that's the tree there we'll have to convince," he said, nodding at a tree two over from ours. "The majority of your Elders roost there nights. And while everyone has a say here, those twenty or thirty have more influence than anyone. I'm going to fly over there and introduce myself." And he flew off as well.

There being nothing else anyone felt they could add, we decided to do what everyone decides to do when there's nothing else to be done. Eat.

Kym, Kyf, Kryk and myself, along with about fourteen others from another flock, decided to search for food. As we left the roost, a returning band called that they'd found good eating.

We followed their directions and soon came upon a welcome sight. Maybe fifty or sixty individuals from the Urkana perched in what I came to understand were pecan trees, eating.

I'd eaten pecans before, hidden among human scavenge, but I'd never had any fresh from the branch, so this was a bit of a glorious surprise. Apparently it was late in the season and unusual to find any nuts left on the tree, but there were still a few hanging. I went to ground to forage, however. The ones lying on the grass beneath the tree had grown a little softer and easier to crack, and if you were lucky, you found a tiny, tasty grub coiled around the nut within the casing.

And I have to repeat this — it was a pleasure to eat with Crows from the Urkana. There were so many of them, and they were so organized, that it was possible to relax, eat and still feel absolutely secure.

The eating was of such quality and quantity that I felt only a little disappointed when scouts warned that two humans were approaching. As I prepared to retreat, another group from the Collection abruptly separated out and lifted into the air. I noticed that one of them was larger than most — Kuper.

He and the others began swooping in close to the humans. The humans grunted and barked at first and, when that didn't work, threw rocks and sticks. Kuper's mob easily avoided these and began pecking at the humans.

The humans found that alarming. Within moments they'd turned and fled. I noticed that Kuper was relentless. He kept after the humans right up until they found refuge in one of their moving boxes.

When his band returned to the flock, there was a good deal of self-congratulation and a general air of celebration. "Did you see that? How the humans scattered?" one older fellow near me asked, chuckling to himself. "Like flies from fruit."

This wasn't the first time he'd seen them do something like that, he informed me. Kuper's bunch had chased humans on several occasions, driving them off to allow others at the Urkana to continue feeding. It had raised their esteem in the eyes of many of the flock. I lifted my head to look at Kuper, and a wave of uneasiness passed over me. Apparently, we had his attention, too. I wasn't certain if it was me specifically he was gazing at, but if it wasn't me, it was certainly someone in our little group. Whomever he was staring at he was a subject of much discussion with others in his band.

I turned from him and glanced back toward the end of the field. There, the humans lingered a long, long while inside their moving box, brooding, staring and gesturing silently behind their invisible stones at the Crows flying overhead.

CHAPTER 26

Next morning, only a brief time was allowed for scavenge. We were assembled and ready as the sun rose, and as early as that was, there were already several individuals eager to speak. The first two, it seemed, were undecided, but the third, a frail Elder with bad eyes, from the southwestern mountains, Kree ru Kreewyt, appeared to express the sentiments of many.

"I speak only for myself," she quavered. "The Plague scavenged our flock. We fled fields, perched among the human, were chased. Those already weak from fever or hunger died. The wind blew hard all that long night that my own Clan perished. The Maker was speaking to me, through that wind —

but I, in my grief, was unable to understand. Why would the Maker bring all this terrible change without a reason? It's clear to me now that the wind blew this new one here. Cousins, that wind is gliding through the trees now. Listen. Hear it. It's moving the clouds, stirring the bushes. It carries a blessing for the Collection, and I will listen to these ones."

Kyp had been waiting to speak. Now he flew up.

"My flock will *not* join the Collection," he began bluntly. "We've received that invitation before and declined. Their invitation is the sort the eagle gives the sparrow to come eat — it comes only once. Since we refused to join the Collection, we have flown many, many days to avoid them and have been chased and attacked by them a number of times."

Several among the Urkana stirred when they heard this, and I could see that some were upset.

"His plan seems a bad one to me. To steal from the human in moderation, to use stealth, and above all to *escape* — these are things the Maker has taught us from early times. His intention to recklessly pursue the human seems to counter those teachings and can only lead to tragedy. And I know this Chooser from prior experience. I know he has no respect or regard for flock or tradition. I know he attacked and killed the Chooser of the Kinaar as he lay sick with the Plague. The Urkana is, of course, large enough and wise enough to decide for itself, but I urge all those here to consider carefully what honor is to be found in the shameful murder of an Elder, or what freedom there is in coercion and threats, or what sense —"

I could see he was having an impact upon several Elders, but just as his words left his beak, a flurry of activity interrupted the discussion. Near the base of a tree, two Crows had dropped to the ground and were furiously pecking and clawing at one another. One of them was Kryk.

Kyp dropped to the earth and intervened between the newcomer and Kryk. The newcomer lunged again, and Kyp blocked his path.

"*I* have something to say!" the stranger shouted, as he paced in front of Kyp, trying to slip past him to Kryk. "I am Ur-Ryk ru UrKarak. These new ones come and talk of betrayal, but why is *he* here? Why have they brought him?" And as he finished his question, he quickly hopped up and flew over Kyp's head. Kyp stretched and seized Ur-Ryk by his left leg and yanked him back to earth.

"This one flies with us!" Kyp insisted. "He is a member of our flock, has been given permission to roost and cannot be harmed."

From the ground, Ur-Ryk cried, "This one has *brought* harm. This one has *caused* harm and must be called to judgment."

"He has done nothing while here," Kyp replied, making sure he spoke loudly enough that everyone in the assembly heard. "What harm did he bring?"

"What *harm* did he bring?" Ur-Ryk struggled to his talons. "Did you hear that, everyone? What *harm*? What harm does the snake bring to the nest, or the weasel —"

Ur-Ryk lunged again. Kyp knocked him to the ground and planted himself on top, then turned to Kryk. "Do you know this Crow?"

"No," Kryk replied, shaking his head. "I've never seen him."

"Don't *know* me?!" The Crow surged from the ground again, and again Kyp restrained him and looked to the Elders for direction.

"What should I do with this one?" Kyp called to the branches where the Elders perched. "This flies against all your customs!"

Ur-Kwyt ru Katu ru Kwyt flew down, and four younger Crows followed him. "Stop this at once," he snapped. "This is shameful. Do you understand anything about how to behave? Do you not recall the pledge your Clan gave? Do you know what honor is, or respect?"

"Let me up!" Ur-Ryk shouted. "Let me up!"

Kyp remained where he was. "Are you in control of yourself?" Ur-Kwyt asked.

"Yes," Ur-Ryk answered in a calmer voice. "I'm sorry. Have him let me up."

Kyp released the Crow. Ur-Ryk stood and jerked his head in the direction of Kryk. "*He* says he doesn't know me, but I tell you I know him. Three years ago, my flock was feeding on pecans. We heard the calls of a hurt Crow and flew to see what we could do." He turned and glared at Kryk. "It was *him*."

"You're sure?" Ur-Kwyt demanded.

"I could not be more sure. He was lying on the ground. He called many times. We circled and then flew down to find out what help we could provide. As we approached the ground, three humans hidden in the grass raised stingers and killed twenty of our flock. Those that survived flew away in confusion, but later I returned to see if there were any of our folks who might be rescued. Instead, I saw this one. Perched on the shoulder of a human. Being fed."

The flock fell deathly quiet. Ur-Kwyt approached Kyp.

"You Choose for your flock," he said quietly. "Can you vouch for this one?"

"I've never heard anything like this." Kyp turned to Kryk. "Does any of this make sense to you?"

Kryk's head rotated to face the Elder, then rotated back to look at Kyp, then lifted to look up at Kym.

"Well?" Ur-Kwyt demanded.

"I was captured by the human," Kryk answered quietly.

"Speak up."

"I was captured by the human," Kryk repeated in a louder voice. "I was forced to call." He faced Kyp. "I didn't want to."

"Forced to call," Ur-Kwyt repeated. "So, is it true what he said? That Crows were killed when you called for help?"

"Yes."

"And after? Did the human feed you after?"

"Yes."

That single word hung in the air. It was as if all other sound had been banished.

"How many times did you do this?"

"Many."

"*How* many?"

"I don't know."

"Once?" Ur-Kwyt snapped. "More than once? Ten times —"

"The human," Kryk began miserably, "would leave his roost to kill maybe five times a year."

The Urkana gasped.

"How many years were you with the human?" Ur-Kwyt asked.

"Six."

"So you helped him kill your own kind on as many as thirty different occasions?"

"Helped him?" Kryk repeated, his voice growing shriller. "I didn't *help* him. I did what I had to do to survive. What else was I supposed to —"

"Was it," Ur-Kwyt interrupted, "thirty times or not?"

"It might have been more. I don't know."

The Urkana perched silently. No one said a word. The wind stirred the grass.

"I want to say," Kryk began again, "that I apologize. I was raised by the human. I didn't know how to behave. Since then, I was freed and have flown with Kyp's flock and am just learning, learning ... learning everything, really. What it means to —"

"This is," Ur-Kwyt said stiffly, "unprecedented. I've never heard anything like it. We must stop and consider things. We will call a recess." He turned away and flew from the glade. As soon as he had departed, the others on all the branches left their perches. We retreated to the tree we had been using as a roost.

"What is all this about?" Kyp asked, turning on Kryk. "Why didn't you tell us?"

"I meant to."

"*Meant to?*" Kyp fumed. "You had plenty of time if you meant to —"

"I wanted to, but —"

"He told me," Kym interrupted.

"What?" Kyp turned to look at Kym.

"He told me. Back when we were still flying from the Collection."

Kyp stared at her, speechless.

"And you didn't think we should know?" he asked finally.

"I told him that we'd let everyone know when we'd reached the Gathering Tree. I thought that would be ..." — she trailed off — "a better time. I'm sorry."

"Well. It's late to find out now," Kyp snapped. "Any influence I had with the Urkana has vanished. And it may take all of us a considerably longer time to get to the Gathering Tree. If we can get there at all."

"It's not her fault," Kryk broke in. "I begged her not to tell. It's my fault. Is there anything you can do? Anything?"

Kyp perched, looking out at the thousands of others perched, knowing that they were all discussing the same thing. "I don't know," he answered quietly. "I'll do what I can."

When everyone assembled again, however, you could sense that the mood had changed. The Urkana appeared to listen impassively as Kyp stepped forward and began to address them. "I didn't try to keep anything hidden from all of you," he explained. "I just learned about this, this moment. I apologize for the upset it has caused and understand how anxious it would make you. It's true, Kryk was raised by the human. It would seem that the human required terrible things of him. But remember his age, and remember when he was first taken by the human. He had barely learned to fly. He knew almost nothing but what the human taught him. If we are trained a certain way from the time we are hatched, can anyone be surprised if we obey? Wouldn't it be more surprising if we didn't? I can say that since he has flown with us, Kryk has flown as a good member of the flock. He truly knows very little about what it is to be a Crow. But he is trying — I see that every day. He is trying very hard. Back in the earliest First Times, when Great Crow stole Sun Eagle, we're told the Maker forgave him. Now, Kryk asks our forgiveness. Can we do any less?"

No one flew forward to argue, and at first I thought that Kyp had somehow managed to per- suade the flock. Had managed, miraculously, to change everyone's minds. Then I realized that there was no one, virtually no one, outside our flock, who was willing to speak on behalf of Kryk. I understood that they had made up their minds and that the discussion was, for all intents and purposes, over.

I desperately tried to think of something I could say or do that would change minds, but came up empty. I could see Kym, Kyf, Kuru all arriving at the same conclusion. I was taken by surprise when Kyf suddenly leaped to a branch. "Deadly?" she de- manded. "Dangerous?" She cast her eyes upon Kryk.

"Why, Kryk is as deadly as last year's eggshells. I have been watching over him, flying after him and keeping his beak out of the hornet's nest since he joined us, and I don't know when I've seen a more pathetic creature. He is the worst, absolutely the worst, flier I have ever seen. The worst scavenger. The worst everything, really."

She paused for a moment to catch her breath, and I realized how high her emotions were running, how much she invested in the safety of each individual in our flock. She gathered herself, craned her neck and gazed out at the assembly. "Do you honestly think the human wouldn't have found ways to kill us without this one? The *human* — who has found an infinity of ways to destroy us already." She shook her head, as though shocked at their credulity. "The human, the human. Maker in the Nest, but you're all fond of talking about the human. The human brought us the *Plague*. The human has cut down our *trees*. The human! I will tell you *this*. The human is responsible for a good bit of tragic nonsense, here and elsewhere, but our failings, the nonsense we perform *ourselves*, the nonsense we do without even knowing it's nonsense — well, if you ask me, that'll be the death of us. More than the Plague. More than the human, Cousins, it's us and how we treat one another. And when I hear you talking, it's as plain as the beak on my face. Can you change the human? No. Can you fix it? Bring it back to the Maker? You know you can't. The only thing you can bring back is yourselves. Bring yourselves back. Bring yourselves back, find your own way there, because if you don't, well, if you don't …" — she looked around at the assembly — "… you're lost, aren't you? You're lost and I don't know how you'll find your way to the roost."

And she withdrew. And as she flew back to her perch, I heard Kuru mutter, "Well. Seems we have at least one Crow here."

"The accusation is of endangering the flock," Ur-Kwyt pronounced, and I understood that we had moved directly to judgment, without any further preliminaries. "Are we agreed?"

With the exception of our band, the flock returned a loud and unanimous "Yes."

"How do you answer?" Ur-Kwyt demanded of Kryk.

"You ask me to answer," Kryk replied, casting his eyes around at the Elders. "I was raised by the human. That's my only answer. I did what the human trained me to do. You may think it's not possible to change. But I have. These ones here helped me escape from the human. I've found a place with them, and they have been teaching me. They know I've changed. Ask them. I'm different now. I'm different. I am not the Crow I was."

Ur-Kwyt waited until Kryk had finished, then flew to the branch beside him. I knew as soon as he grasped the perch how things would fall. "I have discussed this with our council of Elders. The judgment," he pronounced, and I saw Kryk flinch, "of the Urkana is Banishment. No contact. No assistance. Your name stricken from conversation. Fly, and never return. Never greet us. Never let your flight cross ours. Any who find you, any who see you, any who discover your presence, have the right to kill you." He turned from Kryk. "Now go."

And throughout the trees, Crows up and down did likewise, turning their backs to him. Only our flock remained facing Kryk. He crouched, trembling, his chest heaving. He glanced briefly at us and scanned our eyes. "Sorry," he whispered. Then he lifted his wings and flew.

CHAPTER 27

"I never would have taken you for a speaker."

Kuper woke with a start. He peered through the darkness and saw Kym perched on the branch next to him, her wings folded. "As I recall, you always kept to yourself," she said.

"How did you get here?" he asked, clearing his throat and glancing about to determine who had failed to keep watch.

"I walked," Kym answered.

The big bird squinted at her and tried to shake the unease that her appearance provoked in him. "*Walked?*"

"From our perch, along that rough line of shrubs," she explained, nodding to the ground below. "Your scouts were looking in the wrong direction."

Kuper blinked. "I suppose they never expected a Crow to scamper through the dust. You've turned into a groundling since I last saw you," he said and chuckled. Then he turned his attention to the Crows out at the edges of the tree. "I'll have a talk with them later."

"But," Kym said as she settled the primaries of her wings, "there's no reason why we can't discuss things while I'm here, is there?"

"Of course not. But the watch should know when they have been negligent." He glared at the Crows at the tree's outer edge one more time, then reluctantly turned his attention back to Kym. "You haven't changed much since I last saw you."

"Nor you," Kym replied.

"Thank you. I understand you were captured by the human as well."

"That's right."

"I was sorry to learn of it. I know what that's like," Kuper said, giving her an appreciative glance. "Congratulations on your escape."

"I couldn't have done it without Kyp. You know that, don't you? He found me. He freed me."

Kuper said nothing. The silence among the branches grew.

"I don't know all that has happened since I last saw you," Kym said at last, "or what's passed between Kyp and you — I don't understand it — but is it possible for us all to put it behind us?"

Kuper preened a moment and then cocked his head.

"You've walked here for a reason," he said, changing the subject. "What can I do for you?"

Kym straightened on the perch. "May I speak plainly?"

Kuper gave a nonchalant shrug. "You should speak however you wish."

"Things can't be going the way you'd planned. It's clear you meant to stop Kyp before he connected with the Urkana. That didn't work. You tried to intercept him and all of us again back north. You couldn't. He beat you here, and he has beaten you all along. It's not too late to reconsider."

Kuper seemed to focus on the birds beyond the tree. "Those," he said evenly, "are the words of someone who today saw the assembly lose all confidence in Kyp."

"And poor, poor Kryk," Kym reflected bitterly. "The way you used his own terrible situation to turn the assembly against Kyp is, I think, one of the more shameful things you've done so far."

"He helped the human kill Crows," Kuper replied coldly. "Whatever happens to him now is better than he deserves."

"There's not much forgiveness in you," she noted.

"The time for that kind of thing is past."

The two regarded each other from their mutual perches. "So, there's nothing Kyp can do?"

The very thought that there might be seemed to leave Kuper with a bad taste in his beak, but at last he spoke. "Tell him to leave," Kuper permitted. "If he slips away in the night, without explanation or a word to anyone. If he leaves, now. You and the rest can join us and call it fair."

"He'll never do that," Kym responded matter-of-factly. "And I don't think there is anyone in our flock who would join you. Is there anything else?"

Kuper studied the darkness.

"Nothing?" Kym inquired again. "Really nothing? We were all three of us friends once." After she received no reply, she whetted her beak against a branch. "Well. I thought it was worth a try."

"He abandoned both of us, you know," Kuper said quietly. "And it was only an accident that he found you."

Kym lifted her beak and peered sidelong at Kuper over the end of it. "Have you ever heard of Kallu?"

Kuper shook his head.

"He was a Crow back in First Times who became angry because he felt chickadees were too noisy. He wasn't fast enough to catch them, though, or fierce enough to scare them, so he decided that he would just eat everything they ate. He reasoned that when there was nothing left, they would be forced to leave. So, he set about eating all their food — seeds, cones, husks. He didn't like it much, but he kept at it. And, eventually, the chickadees fled. Elated at his success, he looked around and saw other creatures he didn't care for. He didn't like larks either — too noisy — and he figured what worked before could work again. This time he ate bugs and beetles. The larks left, too. Naturally, Kallu hated owls worse than anything. What did owls eat? Crows. So, Kallu started eating his talons, moved to his legs and finally ate every single part of himself except his beak. And when he got there, he said 'Finished at last.'"

"A nice story," Kuper remarked.

"You're on the way to eating your talons now, Kuper. Keep on and I'm sure in the end you'll be able to say, along with Kallu, 'Finished at last.'" The two perched quietly. "I'll return to my roost, then," Kym said.

"Wait," Kuper began as she turned to go. She stopped. "Did he send you?"

"No," she answered, "he doesn't know I'm here. No one does."

Kuper stared intently at her. "You tell me it's not too late to reconsider, but that cuts both ways. There's a new wind blowing. If you don't fly with it, it will knock you out of its way." He looked directly at her. "It's not too late to join me."

"Oh, Kuper," she said sadly, "it was too late for that so long ago. It was too late before I was even captured by the human." She brought up her wings. "Good eating," she concluded simply and nodded, then dropped from the branch.

CHAPTER 28

After Kryk's Banishment, the assembly carried on as though he had never been there. As though he had never even existed. With this exception: *our* words were now tainted. It was impossible to mention Kyp without, in the same breath, also mentioning Kryk.

In our own flock, our thoughts often turned to Kryk. Kym and Kyf especially felt his loss. Late at night, I'd look at the dust settling and wonder where he was. How he would survive. For Kyp, who had been so intent about bringing everyone to roost, it seemed to firm something up within him. He didn't mention Kryk, but there were many times I saw him staring off worriedly in the direction Kryk had flown.

When we assembled again, one of the eldest in the flock, Ur-Kwanyt ru Korlu ru Kwu, a Crow of thirty-five years and considerable stature, gestured that he wished to speak. Kuru had already informed us that he was one of the most influential in the flock because of his age, the position he had among the southern families and the respect his Clan held. So we'd been encouraged that he hadn't spoken yet, supposing that anyone who had hesitated to speak up till now was waiting because they were sympathetic to our view.

He settled, perched and spent a long time adjusting himself before saying anything.

"The wind has mighty wings," he commenced in a frail, thin voice. "She flies over mountaintops, slips through forests, enters deep into burrows. The wind is a prodigious traveler, Cousins, and when she comes to roost, *this* is where she perches."

He cast his eyes across the southern horizon. "Those clouds there — she builds her nests among them. When she flies in strength what can prevail against her? Grasses bow, tall trees snap, the earth groans, is cracked and carried where she will as dust. The wind is among us today, my Cousins. She is speaking with us. When she comes in strength, she brings change. Spring rains. The blizzards of winter. These strangers, these fliers with the Collection have invoked the wind, and I tell you a change is coming. We cannot flee. We cannot hide. And we will not survive resisting it. However it has happened, these strangers fly on the back of that wind, and I for one will not oppose them."

Kyp shook his head, reflecting what we all felt, that with this pronouncement, we had lost a critical portion of the flock. We knew that many, many in the Urkana — even if they agreed with us — wouldn't speak against Ur-Kwanyt out of respect for his age and position, but Kuru seemed almost ready to burst.

He leaped to the ground and began speaking at once. "Well, that's just the most —" he raged, then shook himself and tried to start again in a calmer manner. "I've heard you talk at nightfall and *thought* you had sense. I *thought* you held our ancestors in reverence. I *thought* you spoke with the restraint, care and reflection that come with your age and position, but by the Maker I'm telling you that on this matter you know nothing — less than nothing. There's no more care, or concern, or foresight, or wisdom, or vision, or perception — in short, no more *thought* — in what you had to say than there is sense in stone. Aren't you ashamed to speak? Aren't you the least bit ashamed?" And he snapped his head about to search the crowd for Kuper. Finding him, he took a short hop in his direction. "And you! You come here with all your talk, and all your friends, and your followers, and your plan. Your precious *plan*." He snorted a bitter, dismissive chuckle. "But what are you? Useless! All you are is afraid. And it's not so bad to be afraid, but you can't plan your life around it and you certainly can't expect us to follow you on the basis of it."

Kuru took a deep breath and struggled to control his temper. "Never mind, never mind," he repeated after exhaling and then scowled at the flock again.

"I have thirty-five years," he called in a louder voice, "as many as Ur-Kwanyt, and I'm asking — who here is a *Crow*?" No one offered a reply. "I'm asking, because I see several kinds of beggar birds here today. Birds who think they deserve something, that they should open their beaks like chicks in a nest, and the Maker will drop some dainty in." He glanced darkly about at the surrounding trees.

"You think life should be *easy*? Well? Do you? You think it should be nice, you should have perches well out of the wind, food laid out for you near the tree? Less snow, more sun? Is that it? Oh what's this? There's no promise of that? Oh then, dear me, it must be the *human*. The Plague has come. Oh me, it's the *human*. Cousins, there has always been trouble! Look about, there's death, and disaster, and fear and flight every day. If you keep your eyes open and your head up, there is a chance, but only a chance, that you will be permitted to stay alive another day. That's the promise the Maker made us, and the *only* promise the Maker has ever made. You give thanks if you have lived through to nightfall because, believe you me, there are many, many creatures who haven't — and some of them you've probably eaten."

"Are you," Ur-Kwyt inquired icily, "finished?"

Kuru's feathers rose and he glared at Ur-Kwyt. "Finished? Maker in the Nest — *no*, I'm not *finished*. You've allowed others to jabber on and jabber on and never a word to stop them in their nonsense, and I am telling you this is too important and I will *not* be silenced. I have as many years as almost any in this gathering, more years than you, and I will have my *say*!" Startled at this explosion, Ur-Kwyt stepped back. Kuru drew in another deep breath, readjusted his tail feathers and continued speaking.

"I've heard more than I care to in this life or the next about the wind. The wind, the wind. The wind," he sniffed. "Cousins, the wind is im-portant. We're told that the wind is the very breath of the Maker. It is the thing that moves us and in turn permits us movement. But we are born in a *tree*. And each night when we sleep, it is to the tree we return. The tree, Cousins, more than anything else in all of the Maker's creation, is *who we are*. It is the foundation of all our traditions and customs, the trunk and the roots. You speak of the wind, but

I ask you now — when you go to sleep, will the wind support you? Will the wind shelter you? Can you raise your chicks, and they theirs, and all the generations to come, on the wind?

"You can't, Cousins," he said sadly. "You can't. I perch here and I tell you — especially you older ones — to your face that if you wrongheadedly pursue things as this chickling suggests, your life has no roost and no roots — no more *tree* — than that bald patch of prairie out there. And before long, you will find that out for yourself.

"And *you*," he said, turning about slowly on his bad hip to face Kuper, "before the Maker, and before all these others as my witness, I tell you that I pity you. Because the wind you prize so highly has talons and a beak, too — and my eyes aren't everything they should be, but already I can see your carcass picked clean by it."

CHAPTER 29

Kyp looked exhausted as he perched with the others on the tree. As he clung to the branch, leaning on his longer right leg, I was struck by how much he reminded me of some other time. Then I recalled how he had looked when we had first escaped from the human's roost, his feathers singed and his insides scorched. I realized in that instant how little time he had been given to recover and heal.

I'd come to understand that Crows of the Urkana thrived on talk almost as much as they did on scavenge. The passionate debate of the day had given them plenty to turn over, and they had called for another night of reflection prior to the discussion the next day. After we had returned to our roost, I think Kyf said it for all of us when she asked, "Is there anything we can do that we haven't done?"

Kyp didn't look up. "I'm not sure," he said slowly. "I feel more certain I should never have let them Banish Kryk. I should have stayed by him."

"No," Kuru said and shook his head. "You couldn't. They'd have fought you, they were that upset. They'd have fought you, and you would have lost. And then we wouldn't be having this conversation."

"He's right," Kym agreed. "The way things turned out, you couldn't have done anything else. And who knows? Kryk may be better equipped to survive than he thinks, or any of us thought. He managed to survive the Plague, and the human. He'll forage out on his own for a time and we'll find a way to collect him when we fly north."

"You either Choose for yourself, and then things are easy," Kuru rumbled. "Or you Choose for the flock. And then it's a hard, uncertain flight."

"It still comes down to what we can do next," I pointed out.

Kyp shook his head. "We have until morning. Perhaps with some sleep, I will know how to explain to these Elders. How to explain to them, and make them understand —"

"Explain?" Kuru interrupted. "What are you going to explain that you haven't already? My grandmother used to say, 'You can sing to a rock but you won't make it love you.'" He turned. "Well, you've sung to the rock, nephew. And it doesn't love you."

Kyp stared at Kuru. "What are you suggesting?"

"Just this," Kuru answered slowly. "I've fought, bickered and frittered away most of my useless life till no flock would have me — till you came along. And maybe the Maker has given me this one chance to put my nest in order." He glanced in the direction of the Urkana. "These old ones aren't stupid, but they're scared. They're so badly frightened by the Plague they can't see straight, and it has them making choices that are just plain wrong."

He shook his head as he considered the day's events. "I was deliberately rude today — which, granted, doesn't come very hard for me. I needed to wake these Elders up. Now, I can delay these proceedings and stretch the discussion out for a good many days yet, but I'm not going to turn them around any more than you have. You've done everything you could to convince the Urkana, but that season has come and gone. It comes down to this — you'll have to break their rules and fly. If not tonight then as soon as you can. If you wait much longer, you may never have to wait again."

He opened his beak to say something else, but then shut it. He closed his eyes and took a deep breath. Kyp moved closer to him on the branch.

"Uncle, are you all right?" he asked. "You look tired."

"Oh, tired," Kuru snorted, raising his head and opening one eye. "Tired? What's that? That's nothing. I'll show these others what *tired* is. I'll make them so tired before I'm done they'll wish they'd never hatched. If you think I was sharp today, you haven't heard anything. But first I'm going to get a little rest. Have myself a bit of a talk-about with some of these oldsters. See if we can put our arguments aside for the moment and pick over the juicier remains of a few of the older stories."

He nodded to all of us. "Good eating," he said and dropped from the branch. He glided to the hoary, ancient hickory tree that had been adopted by some of the Eldest elders for a roost. He was greeted and welcomed in as friendly a fashion as you could have imagined.

That night, the wind bent the trees almost double. I fell asleep listening to its rustling, restless voice, wondering if it had any particular message to deliver to me.

"Come quick!" Kyrt called as he slid under my perch, and the tone he used told me right away that something had gone awry.

"What now?" I thought, my heart dropping as I left my branch and followed him. "What else could possibly go wrong?"

Then he landed at the base of a tree, and I felt all the energy drain from my body. There, sprawled on the grass, was the still, dark form of Uncle Kuru. He had never been the neatest Crow, so as he lay there, his feathers all in disarray, he looked strangely not so very different from how he had in his very untidy, disreputable life.

A crowd of anxious and elderly Crows milled about near his body, individuals Kuru had both befriended and derided since he'd arrived.

"How did this happen?" Kyp asked, as he and Erkala caught up with us and landed next to me.

"Nobody knows," the eldest of the group answered in a quavering voice. "When we woke, there he was." He shook his head. "There he was," he repeated in a quieter voice.

"That's right," one of them said, prodding Kuru a little just to make sure he wasn't going to rise. "What a terrible, terrible shock."

"Did anyone hear him in the night?" Erkala asked. "Did he say anything?"

The Elders shook their heads. "He was old. We know what that's like," one of them observed gently, and others nodded their agreement. "Something happens, something gives — and suddenly you feel weak and release your hold on the branch. Or the wind might have knocked him down."

"Or his heart might have failed while he slept," one of the others suggested. "I've seen that. That speech he gave yesterday was powerful — and he was right! I've been thinking about nothing else since then. That might have done it." He cast a sympathetic glance at Kyp. "He was flying with your flock?"

Kyp nodded. "He'd only been with us a short time."

"I'd just met him," an elderly female reflected, "but he struck me as a fine individual."

The others nodded and made noises indicating their agreement.

"I knew him for a brief time long ago when he flew with my band, before he found and lost his mate," another said. "He was a bit of a hard character to get close to, had a tongue that could scorch the feathers off you —"

"That's true," one of them quietly allowed. "Powerfully sharp tongue."

"— but I don't think I've ever met anyone with more courage or backbone."

As Kyp stared down at the body, I realized how, in a curious way, Kyp had come to rely upon Kuru. "Who will join us in sitting vigil with him?" Kyp asked as he continued looking at the body.

"I will, of course," two of the Elders said simultaneously.

"And I," added another. "In fact, I believe Ur-Kryn has gone to suggest that the assembly be delayed another day out of respect."

"That's good to know. Thank you," Kyp said, his eyes taking in the Elder. "I'll come back with others as soon as I've informed my flock."

On the way back to our roost, Erkala snapped her beak as though she tasted something unpleasant. "Efwyk," she muttered.

"What?" I asked.

"The language of my youth. Anything good to outside appearance but foul inside is 'Efwyk.' This," she grumbled, jerking her head back at Kuru and the Elders, "all this, is Efwyk. It would take a longer fall than that to snap a stiff neck like that old one's. It would take more wind than what blew last night to knock him from his perch. And his heart," she said, giving another dismissive snap of her beak, "from what I could see, was never especially frail."

I hadn't considered the possibility that Kuru's death could be the result of anything but the Maker's own choice. Suddenly I felt cold as we flew.

"Then what?" Kyrt demanded, flying in closer. "You can't believe that one of those Elders would be capable of hurting him?"

"No," Erkala answered, "but would any of them have heard it — with the wind blowing like it did last night — if someone else had? That one I was speaking to now barely heard me, and my beak was nearly resting on his. And," she added, "haven't you noticed how we've got friends wherever we go these days?"

"What do you mean?" I asked.

"Look." She nodded. "There."

I glanced in the direction she'd indicated and saw three Crows some distance away, flying casually and tossing a twig from one to the other.

"What about them?" Kyrt inquired.

"They were flying alongside us when we came out this way."

I watched them a moment. They seemed completely absorbed in their game. "Do you know them?"

"All three," Kyp observed without glancing back at us, "members of the Collection."

CHAPTER 31

"Ow."

I was awakened later that night by a sharp peck in the back of the head.

"Shh," Erkala whispered. "Come."

It was still early in the dark sixth of a particularly blustery evening. The moon cast a flickering unreliable light as clouds scuttled across the sky. We flew quietly, and in a few moments I noticed three others flying alongside us — Kym, Kyrt and Kyf. Erkala motioned at the ground and we all dropped to the earth. She cast a cautious glance about and then, concluding we weren't being watched, nudged a branch aside with her wing. Leaning forward, she stepped through a thick mat of brush and disappeared. We followed her, pushing the brush aside as we went.

On the other side of the branches was a narrow, dry streambed that we descended into. The brush rose up over top of it like an impenetrable wing. "Now," she whispered, "we walk through here."

"*Walk* through here?" The moon spilled faint streaks of light through the dense canopy of leaves. By that dappled flickering illumination I could see the streambed wind ahead into a thick, threatening gloom. It was the kind of place I imagined scorpions gathered when they wanted to meet other scorpion companions. "Isn't there another and even scarier way?" I inquired.

"Don't fuss!" Erkala hissed. "Just follow. And quietly."

"Why?" I asked. And very reasonably, I thought. "What's up above this plant cover, that we can't just go that way instead?"

"Over that rise back there," she jerked her beak up, "an owl's nest is being built. Anyone who follows after us above this hidden path will meet up with the bad-tempered and very hungry owner of that nest."

"So, you think we're likely to be followed?" Kyrt asked.

She turned to him. "Don't you?"

The dried streambed twisted and descended. The walls of the ravine rose as we proceeded, and soon the plant canopy was replaced by the inclining surface of wind-polished rock. The way was dark, and pebbles and piles of twigs obstructed the path at times, so it was slow going. At last Erkala chose a narrow side channel that brought us to a tiny circular hollow. We hopped up from the streambed and found perches in the sandstone. Kyp was already there, waiting for us.

"I asked Erkala to guide you here so that we could talk freely. It's no surprise to anyone when I say things aren't going well. Kuper has done much better than any of us suspected he would. Certainly better than I imagined." The moonlight glittered off his eyes as he stopped to consider the past events. "But there's no point worrying about the past. Now we have to make new plans."

"If we stay," Kyf asked, "what can we hope for?"

Kyp thought before answering. "Uncle Kuru — the Maker keep him — was right. Kuper is carrying the Urkana. And not just him; there are members of his Collection who are busy arguing his case whenever the assembly adjourns. His recent raids upon the human have also proved very popular. My feeling is, when time comes to Choose, the Urkana will be divided. The argument may continue late —

maybe for several days more if there is some very deep opposition — but in the end, they'll follow the Collection. And once that happens, we will be asked to obey and join the Collection as well."

Erkala grunted. "And if we don't?"

"We gave our promise to obey while we were here. If we disobey ... well, the Urkana won't force us to become part of the Collection — it's too close to the time when the Urkana would have disbanded anyway, to allow folks to return to their nesting grounds — but I don't think a one of them will stop Kuper and his bunch if they attack us."

"There *has* to be a way out," Kyrt muttered. "Didn't Kwaku say there would be?"

"There were a few things he predicted that would have to happen first," I reminded him. "I haven't been greeted by the dead yet. Have you?"

"There's no helping it," Kyf concluded, "we'll have to do as Kuru suggested and fly."

"Yes, but, if you haven't already noticed," I pointed out, "the Collection is keeping a very close watch. Look how difficult it was for the few of us getting away now."

"Can't we slip away in smaller groups?" Kym suggested.

I thought about the events of the day. "Considering what happened to Kuru," I observed, "I don't think we can assume that that will be easy, or safe."

"None of it will be easy," Kyp declared. "I won't lie to you. When we find a chance — if we find a chance — to escape without anyone noticing, it will mean another long flight, without any certainty."

"Are you telling us," Kyrt asked hesitantly, "that you're giving up?"

"You misunderstand me," Kyp replied. "I'm offering you a chance to replace me."

Nobody said anything. He continued. "I'd understand if you did. I wouldn't blame you."

Kyrt plucked idly at a pebble, turning it over and over, then finally pushing it over the lip of the ledge. "I'm pretty certain my band and I wouldn't have survived the winter if you hadn't found us. So, to my way of thinking, we've already lived one life more than we might have." He looked up at Kyp. "You Choose for us."

"And me," Kym said without hesitation.

"And me," Kyf added.

"Nothing has changed," Erkala said simply. "You Choose."

I found myself thinking through our flight from the time I'd first met Kyp along the lakeshore. The number of cold, damp nights he'd somehow discovered a protected, dry roost when I would have settled for any old, wet perch in the wind. I couldn't see how, even given his talents, he would be able to find refuge for us this time. When I glanced up, I saw that everyone was looking at me and realized they were waiting for me to say something. "It's easy to Choose when times are good. It's when times are bad that Choice counts, and then, Cousins, we are all called to judgment." I shrugged. "There's no reason I can see why we'd want to switch things now."

Kyp looked at each of us carefully and finally nodded. "I felt you should know the risks. But I promise you, on my life, if I continue to Choose, I will somehow find a way to bring us to safety —"

"You can't make that kind of promise," Kym protested. "*Nobody* can make that kind of promise."

"I am *telling* you," Kyp continued, his voice tight, "by the deaths of Kwaku, Kaf, Kuru, and Kalum left to die in the dirt, I brought us here, it's on my head, and I *will* find a way to safe roosting, good eating and the nesting grounds in spring."

Suddenly a shrill, terrible, soul-wrenching cry split the night. We all looked at one another.

"What was that?" Kyf asked.

We hurried back along the path until we came out on the other side of the brush. As we pushed the brush aside, a startled shape separated itself from the darkness and flew off, carrying something in its talons.

"Owl!" Erkala warned.

We stalked cautiously to where the owl had been and found the prone, mutilated body of a Crow.

"It's Kyup," I said, recognizing what was left of his face. "One of the two spies we sent back to the Collection."

"Well," Erkala observed acidly as she prodded the body, "that's the last time we'll be bothered by him."

"Still," Kym said, "you never want to see a Crow end that way. I almost feel guilty knowing that we drew him to this place."

Kyp glanced in the direction of the owl and then at the remains on the ground. "We drew him," he reflected, "and he drew the owl. There may be something we can take from that."

"What's that supposed to mean?" I asked.

"Maybe nothing," Kyp replied. "Only that the things that draw us can also destroy us."

CHAPTER 32

"I remember once, we were many." Kafta ru Kafym, the eldest of the Kwantu Family was addressing the assembly. He had talked for some time, and there had already been fifteen or sixteen such speakers. Although no one had said anything to confirm this, it had begun to feel as if they were summing up. "Then the wind guided us. We flew where she bade and there was always good eating. Those times are past. We peck at sunbaked earth now. Our roosts are exposed to rain and owls. The Plague comes to perch with us, and each year fewer and fewer return to the roost. How many fewer are with us this year? Half? How many fewer will be with us next?"

The lids of his eyes shut, his head hunched in, and when he spoke it was as though recollecting another more distant time. "My bones find comfort when I return to the Urkana. This land knows me. Old friends greet me. I perch in familiar trees, see all these old faces surrounding me. But our times are passing. In my life I have flown over marshes thick with reeds and swamp grass and lilies, through forests that chanted with frogs and crickets under a dark, star-strewn sky. Everything is disappearing. This land. These lives. What will remain? Who will mark our passing? Some counsel this, and others that. I don't fear for myself. What is to fear? Does it matter if we die? What are we but snow? What are we but leaves? What are we but dried grasses lifted and shifted with each passing gust. You others may fly as you will. My wing is with the Collection."

It was customary to catch the eye of one of the Elders and wait to be recognized, but abruptly Kyp flew to the center of the glade, without waiting for acknowledgment or recognition. A ripple of disapproval ran through the Elders.

"I won't keep you," he started without intro-duction. "Others have already spoken more ably than I could hope. And I won't speak about the risk we run if the human comes against us. That *will* happen, can't help but happen. Can you fly into a hive and not get stung? But that's your affair. I *will* speak to what will happen if everything goes well and this plan succeeds — because *that*, I believe, would be the real disaster. If we continue to raid without limit from the human, eat what it eats, abandon migration, move only according to where and when the human provides food, I cannot see how we will avoid becoming a weaker, poorer imitation of the human. Or a kind of slave to the human, like its cats or dogs, without even the meager benefit of the shelter or regular food that its slaves usually are permitted. Others may choose that flight. I won't.

"As for me, I will continue to live as a Crow. And so long as there are even two others with me, I will fly as a flock, migrate, nest, raise chicks and teach them to live as Great Crow did.

"And even if what was suggested wasn't a bad idea — and it is — I would no more follow Kuper — or Urku, as he calls himself — and his Collection than I would roost with owls. His murder of an Elder in my flock took from this world a Crow worth a thousand Kupers. He perches there and tells us not to be afraid, but I can see into his heart and it is eaten up with fear.

"Well. I won't say any more. We are not rats or pigeons to paw and peck after the human wherever it walks. We have wings, Cousins, and were made to travel. We are Crows, Cousins, and it is time we left."

And he leaped up and began flying. As he withdrew, an angry murmur arose from those perched in the trees.

"You have not asked permission to leave!" Kuper shouted.

"These *others* I may ask permission," Kyp snapped as he wheeled about, able as usual to turn on the tightest point I have ever seen. "You," he spat, "I ask nothing!"

The tension, already high, instantly shifted to a still higher level. Kuper might have waited to see if Kyp truly intended to leave and then left it to the Urkana to sort out, but a direct insult, in front of the others, was more than Kuper could bear. Feathers standing straight up, he lunged from his perch. Although Kuper was nearly twice the size of Kyp, Kyp easily outmaneuvered this first attack. Kuper recovered, circled back and struck again, but I have never seen a prettier or more subtle turn than the one Kyp executed. Kuper meant to knock him to the ground and instead struck air. Then two quick hits from Kyp, and Kuper was sent reeling. Kuper was uninjured, but the effect was that he became blind with rage.

In that moment, I saw just how clever Kyp had been. The majority of the Urkana was growing more and more agitated by this open breach of custom. Elders in every tree called for Kuper to stop, and with each call for order that Kuper disobeyed, you could feel the sympathy for the Collection waning.

The truth was that Kuper could attack all he wanted, but he would *never* catch the faster, more agile Kyp. Kuper succeeded only in looking foolish in front of everyone.

Beginning to understand how things were deteriorating, Kuper shouted to his flock, and three other Crows quickly joined him. They didn't attack Kyp, but flew along an outside line to prevent Kyp from escaping. Kyp had warned us ahead of time that he might try something unusual at this assembly and that we should allow it to play out. Nevertheless, overcome by this unfair advantage, Kyrt flew to Kyp's assistance. Several more from the Collection leaped up to stop him, and, outraged by their intervention, four of Kyrt's companions launched themselves.

Some shouting, some flying, some fighting — the assembly seemed on the verge of disintegrating into chaos. Through them all, Kyp coiled and twisted.

"Shame!" a chorus of older Crows called after Kuper. "Shame!"

Even I, who should have known better, threw Kyp's warning aside and joined the brawl.

Kuper made another vicious slash. Kyp adeptly avoided it, then banked right, sweeping low under the bottommost tilting branches of a nearby tree. Because he was chased so closely, because there was so much noise and activity, his attention stayed behind him, and so he was unaware of the massive human box that suddenly hurtled around a corner.

All we saw was the blue-gray blur. All we heard was the sound of Kyp's body striking the rock-hard surface. Then there was silence, and his feathers drifted to the earth.

CHAPTER 33

We gathered for vigil in the branches of the tree above where Kyp fell. Kym and Erkala arrived early, but soon the rest of the flock came. I was surprised to see many of the Urkana silently take their place on the branches as well. When the dark sixth arrived and the sun was poised like a blood blister on the edge of a red and angry horizon, I took my position and began.

"The thing you must recall," I called to those who perched in the trees that afternoon, "is this, Cousins. No one ever wants to leave.

"The Maker flew over Earth shortly after she had made it and saw that it was already becoming too crowded. No matter how she invited the others, no

246

one was willing to leave. Because, just as we are gluttons for food, Cousins, we are gluttons for life. We can be completely full to the brim and still not have had enough. So what did the Maker say?"

The flock replied, "The Maker told them, come. As you were first to be created, you will be first to leave. Come with me. You will find good eating. The roost I have is dry and out of the wind."

I nodded. "But even the Maker can make a mistake. The Maker didn't know, couldn't understand, that when she made Crows, we would grow so fond of Earth and each other. No matter how the Maker invited us, no matter how she cajoled, or what delicacy she offered us, Great Crow always had an excuse to delay things. So one evening the Maker made her final creation. She shaped it from the night wind and the keen edge of the falcon's talons. She made it from the muffled sweep of the owl's wing and the bitter pang of a failing, ailing heart. And when it was ready, she whispered to it, 'You are the fastest of my creations, and the most tireless. You are Death and you will take many forms. Chase Crows, and when you catch them, eat them.'

"And since that time, the snake has wound his way up the trunk, the fox has pounced through the bush blind. Weasel and lynx and hawk and owl pursued us, and there were diseases that chased us as well. And when the Maker saw that her creation was successful, she released it on all other living things, and all of life became acquainted with death.

"Even so." I took a deep breath and continued, "Even so, Great Crow was cunning. He led his flock, and wherever he encountered a difficulty, he also had a plan. He learned to circle three times before he perched. He learned to call warning when there was danger and to sleep on the tree's limb with one eye open. And though some were caught, and some were eaten, and some were sent along their way by disease, still Great Crow guided his flock safely. And though the numbers diminished, the flock still thrived. Though death was quick, Great Crow was quicker.

"And then one cold morning, early, he heard something climbing quietly up the tree and he asked who it was. He was half deaf at this point, so he almost didn't hear the soft, calm voice say, 'I am Time. There is nothing that can outfly me. Nothing.' And Great Crow knew that death had at last taken a form that even he could not escape.

"That is the Maker's message to us. Everyone, at last, must answer her invitation. And now there are many things large and small that chase us from the nest. And many things seen and unseen that can strike us, catch us, choke us and bite us."

For a moment the emotion rose so intensely within me that I thought I could not continue, but as I saw Kym perched straight and dignified, I found strength as well.

"But where," I asked, "is Great Crow now?"

"On another perch," the flock replied.

"Who roosts there with him?" I asked.

"The Maker," they replied, louder.

"What will we find when we join them?"

"Good eating."

"That's right, good eating, Cousins. And the coolest water to quench our thirst and a warm and gentle wind under our wings, which will carry us where the perch is soft and the roost safe. And who has joined the Maker this evening?"

"Kyp ru Kurea ru Kinaar," came the whispered response from all around me.

"That's right," I said. "This day, our Chooser has himself been Chosen, and Kyp ru Kurea ru Kinaar perches with the Maker."

CHAPTER 34

It is impossible to describe how I felt.

Everyone is responsible for their own flight. We awake to life on this side of the shell, and from that time on we choose how and where we will roost. But some individuals bring something extra to your life. They bring light and clarity and meaning. When they go, it is as though the day is diminished. Who had brought us across the land? Who had kept us safe and found a thousand different solutions to avoid disaster? Who had entertained me and put up with me when I was difficult? Who had invited me out of a life of Banishment?

I know that a flock is more than the sum of its individuals, but it is hard to overestimate the value of the individual as well. When I considered the loss of my friend, I felt as though my heart would burst and didn't know if I could carry on.

I returned to the spot where his body was destroyed. His form had already been scavenged by groundlings, but feathers still lingered and floated along the hard-packed human trackway and among the tall grasses that bordered it. I lifted a quill and felt the absence of the Crow it had once adorned. In that moment, the weight of that single feather was almost too much for me to bear.

I lowered my head and shook the glitter from around my neck. It dropped to the ground, rolled and settled in the dust. What use glitter anymore? Then I closed my eyes and allowed the wind to sweep through me.

Kyp's plan had worked, of course. Kuper and the Collection were held in disgrace and completely isolated from the Urkana. The proceedings of the Urkana had been indefinitely delayed. The Urkana sent a large number of Crows to separate our flock out from Kuper's and prevent any incidents.

Kym perched alone in a tree, seemingly unable to move. Kyf tried several times to organize the flock, but halfway through she would become distracted and forget what she was doing. Kyrt and his bunch huddled in a tree together, silent and still.

I had to ask myself, What would Kyp do under these circumstances? And I knew. He would quietly be organizing things. He would be encouraging others. He would be trying to develop a plan, then developing another in case the first didn't work. He would search for food and a safe, comfortable roost. He wouldn't let the flock simply drift about.

I couldn't do these things.

I couldn't. Not on my own — but if I thought about what Kyp would do, then I was able.

I approached Kym and asked her if she would accept Choice for the flock. She seemed surprised, but shouldn't have been. She was the only other one the confined would follow, and the rest of the flock thought highly of her. No one else had wings long enough to lift and bear us. Once she had accepted her position, I offered my assistance and began to gather our folk. Then Kym gave the Call and we moved to a tree off on our own.

Erkala approached the assembly and requested permission to leave. She was the first to do so formally, but others followed not long after. I flew alongside Erkala and quietly urged her to reconsider. Shouldn't she, I asked her, at least spend some additional time with us grieving?

"Grief will find its own time," was her characteristically enigmatic response — and then she left. I was bitterly disappointed, and hurt, but not surprised. It was Kyp and the force of his character that had kept us together, after all.

As Erkala flew away, however, I felt a pang of uneasiness that accompanies a particularly bad decision, and I regretted letting her leave as easily as I had. Although Kuper was completely disgraced in front of the Urkana, I couldn't help but worry that he might still find some way to harm her. I hesitated a moment, then flew after her.

She had a considerable head start, and I might not have caught up with her at all had she continued directly, but for some reason she doubled back. I saw her and the yearlings accompanying her curl back and then disappear into a sandstone gully.

I halted a moment. She would have known better than anyone the risk of remaining in the vicinity. What could possibly be down the gully that would prompt her to linger?

I leaned into the wind, banked left and entered the ravine.

As the stone walls rose on either side of me, I caught the last trailing glimpse of tail feathers slipping around a winding corner. I followed, and as I did was abruptly dropped upon. Unable to support the weight, I plummeted to the ground and quickly found my beak planted in the dust.

"Mites in the Nest!" I cursed as I struggled to

dislodge the body from my back. "Get off me! What's this all about?"

"Kata?" a surprised voice asked.

The Crow stepped off me. As I climbed to my talons, I saw Erkala standing in front of me, bristling. "Why were you following us?" she demanded.

"Do you have to ask?" I fumed. "Haven't we been pursued and ambushed at every roost and perch of our journey? I was worried about you. I just wanted to make sure that none of Kuper's —"

And then I saw. Perched on a thorny bush at the bottom of the defile was a familiar face.

"Kyp!" I cried.

"Shh," Erkala hissed.

I ignored her protests, flew past her to the branch where he perched and stared. I opened and shut my beak uselessly a number of times before I was finally able to ask, "Is it you?"

"Yes."

"*How*? I saw your body —"

"The body of Kyup, the Crow who had spied on us the previous night. I'd cached it earlier. Erkala pushed it from a branch in front of the moving box, I slid under as the moving box swept past and then hid in a hollow at the base of a tree till dark."

"His body?" My mind raced to the time of our secret meeting. "Of course." I glanced at Erkala. "And that's the reason why Erkala and the others have begun leaving as well — to join you. But, but, that plan was *completely* dangerous. You could have been killed any number of times, crushed by the moving box, discovered and set on by Kuper and those others — why didn't you tell me?"

"I couldn't afford to tell you, Kata. *They* had to believe, truly believe, I was dead if we were to have a chance of getting away. Not just Kuper but all of the Collection and the Urkana. You're such an honest individual, it's always been easy to see how you felt." Kyp stepped closer. "I left the hard work to you and Kyrt to convince the rest of the flock that I was truly dead. I'm sorry."

"And you should be," I snapped. "Not feeling you can trust *me*! *Who* has been with you longer than anyone else? *Who* has flown with you and stuck by you? Who...?" I closed my beak and tried to get some control of my temper. "I don't know if I'm more *angry* at you or frustrated or ..."

I couldn't think of anything else to say. I shook my head and squinted at him again. "Nest of the Nest, it's good to see you again," I muttered finally, then drew a breath and tried to settle my scattered thoughts. "Now what?"

"Now we leave. Some of you will fly tomorrow. If the rest of you slip away in smaller groups, the Urkana won't even notice. They'll simply continue thinking I'm dead and believe it's grief that guides you. I'm afraid the last to leave will have to be Kym to keep those remaining few organized."

"When do I follow?"

"You'll have to stay with Kym and help her. Day after tomorrow you should be able to join us. So, you'll have to return to the Urkana — and try *not* to look as pleased as you do now."

That was harder to accomplish than I thought it would be. This completely unexpected good news had caught me so off guard that I had to force myself to recollect several fairly sad memories just to shift to happy from giddy and exultant.

As I was about to leave, I found Erkala perched in front of me.

"So," she inquired archly, "you were worried about me?"

"Never mind that," I retorted, dismissing her with a curt wave of a wing. "Don't think that I've forgotten or forgiven *you*. You, at least, could have done something, hinted something. You could have whispered *something* to me about all this. Really, I'm not sure that I'm even talking to you yet."

"I thought you might be irritated," she said, "so I brought you some scavenge. It's on that bush there." And she flew away.

I glanced over at the bush. On the third branch from the bottom dangled a shimmering hoop — the glitter I'd abandoned in the dust.

CHAPTER **35**

Muted, trailing thunder made the branch beneath Kyp tremble. After the continued threat of rain the previous day, he felt almost relieved to sense the wind picking up and know that a downpour would soon arrive. He scratched himself and pecked absently at the tiny flies that flew about him.

A clatter from the far end of the canyon caught his attention. Kyp cocked his head. Echoes bounced off the canyon walls, making it difficult to say for sure what had generated the noise or where it had come from.

The noise sounded again. Still unable to identify it, Kyp decided to explore further. He followed the winding ravine and finally arrived at the cliffs where, had the streambed not been dry, the creek would have dropped onto the floodplain below. From the dusty stone lip where water would normally have cascaded, Kyp perched in the shadows and watched.

Clouds were piling up thick and heavy throughout the valley. Lightning flickered faintly along the dark southern horizon, and after a short pause, thunder followed. Kyp sniffed and smelled the sharp scent of rain. Among the dense row of bushes that lined the river something stirred.

Kyp hopped along the ridge, moving quietly over rocks, until he was nearly parallel with the spot where he had seen movement.

There, crouched in the brush below, he found them. Four humans. And then, under a separate cluster of bushes, another movement and three other humans.

Thunder growled again, closer. Kyp glanced up at the low-hanging clouds, then back at the humans. Although it was difficult to tell for certain, the humans seemed to be hiding. Only portions were visible through the branches, but in their paws they clutched dark, glinting things that appeared to be stingers. He craned his neck and hopped as close as he dared. For a brief moment he wished that Kym was beside him. She had spent so much time observing humans she would somehow have been able to make sense of the incomprehensible things they did. Why were they in two groups? And why here?

Then he noticed something else. There, among the branches of trees farther down the valley, something hung and swayed. Kyp hopped to the top of a boulder to get a better look.

If a spider the size of a Crow had spun its web, it might have constructed something of this sort. From tree to tree, a thin crisscrossing weave of the finest gossamer was strung. Kyp peered into the thicket. Over on another tree as well, a web quivered in the breeze. And there, beyond that, was another.

His attention returned to the humans — did they have something to do with the web? Could they have produced it? Was it related to their crouching there? It was clear they were waiting for *something*. They sat so still. Grunted in muted tones to one another. Kyp felt a deep sense of anxiety welling up inside. He peered about, trying to determine what made him feel so uneasy. Then he glanced at the trees again and realized exactly where he was. These were the trees designated as fallback roosts. Should something disturb the Urkana at their roost, this was the grove they were to fly to.

He saw a human grasp one of the stingers, slide its paws along it. He heard the cold, stony clicking he had heard earlier. And suddenly it all began to make sense. Quickly, he turned and flew.

CHAPTER 36

I had already been flying hard for some time and was out of breath when Kyp came upon me.

He must have realized the instant he saw me that something had gone terribly wrong. He pivoted, fell in alongside me and asked what had happened. I told him then the full extent of the disaster. How humans had arrived at the roost in three separate moving boxes. How one of the boxes had advanced on two of the Urkana's largest perches, actually pushed the trees over and trampled them underfoot. How scouts had barely approached when humans leaped from the boxes and withdrew stingers. The explosions began moments later. Many of us had barely made the safety of air when Crows closest to the humans began to drop.

"How many?" he shouted.

I gasped for breath. "Many," I told him. "Many."

It might have been worse, I told Kyp, but for the way Kuper and his flock responded. Instead of fleeing as we normally would have, they had immediately attacked the humans. It was difficult to tell how many of the Collection had fallen in that initial rush, possibly thousands, but the ones who made it through to the humans had hurt and frightened them enough that the humans had finally retreated and found refuge in their moving boxes.

"What about our folk?"

"It was impossible to take a full count," I told him, "but most had already escaped. Slipped away earlier in smaller groups as we'd planned. Kym and a few others were still there, so they fled the roost along with the rest of the Urkana."

"And where would they be now?"

"With the others," I replied, "fleeing south, then circling back to the fallback roosts."

Kyp altered his path. "This way!" he shouted. "If we don't follow the river, we may get there before them!" That's when the first rain began to fall.

CHAPTER **37**

Some believe demons can only be met in nightmares. I don't believe that anymore. They exist more closely than we can conceive — just moments away.

Our folk straggled through the rain, injured and frightened, but confident they had left danger behind. They approached the fallback roosts, looking for safety and security and a place to make sense of what had happened. They had no reason to suspect anything.

The first ones encountered the webs strung between branches. Suddenly snatched in mid-flight, plucked from the air, hopelessly tangled in the thin, unyielding cords. They cried to the others for help. Just as their calls were heard and Crows were gathering to investigate, explosions erupted up and down the valley. Blinding bursts of light flashed up from beneath the cover of the willows and tall reeds. Branches of those trees in the backup roost snapped and were sent spinning. Crows were struck as they tried to change direction. Screams of pain and fear arose everywhere as the blasts kept coming.

"Flying's no use!" Kuper bellowed through a beak flecked with foam. "Down! Come down!" And rather than flying up and off, Kuper folded his wings and dropped directly at the humans. In a moment, others of the Collection joined him. The thunder sounded, stingers crackled. Twenty or thirty Crows fell in an instant. More replaced them, and more explosions followed. Kuper landed atop a human, which attempted to bat him away. Another Crow took a position beside him on the human's upraised paw. With one slash of his beak, Kuper cut the human, just under its eyes. The human roared and dropped its stinger.

Kyp and I arrived in the middle of this chaos — desperate, unable to find our own folk, unwilling to leave without them, maddened by the frightened calls of cousins caught in the mesh. Unable to even understand each other over the deafening noise of the explosions to develop any other kind of plan, we cast aside hope and did as the others were doing. We flew at the humans. Kyp found himself directly in front of one large individual just as it raised its stinger. The explosion it released tore apart three poor Crows immediately next to him. I plummeted through the smoke and landed on the back of the human's head. Kyp raced along the length of the stinger and leaped at the human's paws.

We shouldn't have survived. During that desperate confusion and crush, I don't think any of us had any particular hope of survival, but as we struggled, the rain, already blindingly hard, turned to hail. At first only pebble-sized, it stripped trees, bounced off the earth and split against rocks. Now the howls of humans joined the cries of Crows. Crows and humans alike fled for cover — the humans with their paws thrown over their heads, as much for protection from us as the hail.

Jagged streaks of lightning tore the sky apart. The initial torrent of hail paused, as though for a breath, then renewed, surging stronger than before. Walnut-sized this time, the icy pellets popped as they hit, carving craters in the wet earth. The webs strung between branches were dragged down and tattered, shards left flapping in the wind.

Kyp and I flattened ourselves against the cliffs that ran up the valley and huddled beneath a rock outcrop. Below our perch, branches lay in the mud next to the scraps and shards of the human's things and the scattered, battered bodies of dead Crows.

Cold, cut, wet and tired, we sucked air in, in ragged gasps.

Precisely at the time the hail seemed to be halting, the wind and rain picked up. It became impossible to see any distance through a downpour that was driven nearly sideways by a raging wind.

"Now!" Kyp shouted.

I shook my head, not comprehending. "What?"

"Now!" he repeated over the roar of the storm. "Gather everyone together, there won't be any better time. Find whoever you can — I'll do the same — and we'll leave. Fly north. Escape the humans, *and* the Collection and all of this mess once and for all. Look for me along the cliffs of the river valley farther up."

Exhausted as I was, I realized that Kyp was right — if we left now, no one would notice, or be able to follow later. I nodded and flew south.

Kyp launched himself north. The rain drenched him and bore him down. Suddenly, over the scream of the wind and the clatter of water running through drifts of hail, he heard something else. He flew lower, trying to make out what it was. Something. He lifted his head, turned and flew closer to the cliffs. A few more flaps of his wings and he was certain. It was Kym he heard.

He banked right and slipped between two trees. As he turned on his side to negotiate the tight passage, he was suddenly snatched from the air, a sharp pain tracing lines along the outer edges of his shoulders and neck. It was as though his entire body had been seized and squeezed, his wings pinned tightly to his side. He had flown directly into a web.

CHAPTER 38

I labored south, rain streaming into my eyes, calling as I flew. I could only hope that others would somehow hear me over the tumult.

The rain turned to hail again, and I quickly searched for shelter. At the same time, I heard familiar voices. I looked up the valley, and there in the low, dense brush, just off the swollen river, saw Kym, Kyf, Kyrt and a very bedraggled Kymnyt.

"Have you found any of the others?" Kym shouted to me as I dropped beside them.

"Kyp is gathering the rest of the flock up the valley," I called. "He says we're to collect and leave."

"Agreed," Kyf replied, "but first we have to survive this."

The hail pelted harder and I saw a dark shape dropping beside us, the branches bobbing beneath the force of her abrupt landing. Erkala.

"You survived!" I exclaimed. When I'd last seen her she'd been in among the humans and their stingers. Her feathers were uncharacteristically dishevelled, and a ragged patch near her left shoulder seemed burnt nearly bare.

She nodded grimly and briefly tucked her head under a wing to brush water away. "That's more than I can say for many of the Collection. What a waste. Bodies lie everywhere along the cliffs." She skipped back as a particularly large hailstone crashed through the canopy. "It's good to find you, but these bushes won't do. We need stronger shelter."

"What else is there that's close?" Kyf asked, glancing about.

"There!" Kym said and nodded.

Kyf peered through the downpour. "What?"

Kym gestured again. "We can crouch beneath that." Tilted up against the riverbank one of the human's boxes rested, long, rectangular and blood red, hail ricocheting off it. I couldn't see any humans nearby.

"It's the human's —" Kymnyt objected, her tail flicking rapidly. "We'll be caught."

"We won't have to perch long. This hail can't last much longer," Kym said, casting her eyes upward, "then we'll leave."

The branches above us snapped. We took that as a signal and flew.

In the short time it took us to cross that open space, we were all pretty badly bruised. "Quick!" Kym directed. "Under the box." But as I flew beneath, I discovered a torrent of mud, water and ice surging through.

"Won't do!" I shouted to the others as I quickly circled back. "We'll have to go in."

"In *where?*" Kyf shouted, wincing as hail bounced off her wings.

"In," I repeated and lifted my beak. "On the other side of the box the humans have left one entrance open."

Kymnyt shook her head. "Impossible!" she sputtered and suddenly rattled off a frantic stream of foreign-sounding words.

"What?" I shouted.

"Too dangerous!" she yelled. "It's too dangerous!"

A hailstone rapped me sharply on the shoulder. I rolled my eyes. "And what's this?"

Suddenly Kym took a hit on the right wing and grimaced. At the same time, Kyrt was struck between the shoulder blades. He folded and fell without a sound. In a moment he was lying on his side in the mud and running water.

"Kyrt!" I called, tugging on him. "Get up!"

He didn't respond. Kyf leaned in close and began

shouting. "Get up!" she scolded as she prodded him. "You *get up* right now! Stop lying there, you are absolutely *not* allowed to die here. Now get up, get up!"

Miraculously, his eyes fluttered and opened. "All right," he answered weakly. "You don't have to shout."

With some effort he stood. I leaped from the mud into the human box, and the others followed. Once inside, Kyrt collapsed and laid his head flat on the dry surface, panting.

"I can't breathe," he wheezed.

"Stay down. Rest," Erkala urged as she glanced about.

Outside the box, the air itself seemed to turn white as hail came sluicing directly down. Where water wasn't thrusting hail along rivulets and streams, the hail was stacked in heaps two or three Crows high. Suddenly a violent gust of wind rocked the human's box and knocked us flat. Water and half-melted hail washed over us. The stone slab that had been stretched open, allowing our entrance, groaned, shivered and abruptly rushed at us. With a deafening crash, it slammed across the opening, barring the entrance.

We lay a moment, stunned, listening to the furious clatter outside.

"Does that mean," Kyf asked hesitantly, "that we can't get out of here?"

"There must be another way," I assured her, casting my glance about the interior of the box. "Most times these boxes have several entrances."

We quickly flew to different corners of the box.

"Nothing!" Kyf shouted from high up near the top. "Anything over there?"

"No!" I called back after searching the lower reaches.

Then, above the racket of hail, I heard something else. A few flaps took me up to where I could see through the invisible stone. Two humans, their paws stretched up over their heads, charged through the storm toward the box.

"Humans coming!" I warned as I flew to Kyrt's side. "Can you stand?"

"Yes," he answered groggily, rising to his talons.

"Get him back, away from the entrance!" Erkala hissed.

Kyf prodded and shoved him along. We'd only just hidden at the opposite side of the box and crouched near the floor when the humans threw open the entrance. Wind and rain roared in, then the humans leaped to their perches and pulled the slab across the entrance again.

They tossed something heavy behind them, and the sharp, acrid smell of their stingers filled the air. Almost at once we heard a low rumble, the box abruptly lurched, then began to move with us inside.

CHAPTER 39

Kyp dangled and spun one way in the wind — then as the web tightened, corrected and released, it twirled him the other. From his dizzying upside-down position, he was able to make out a Crow perched on a branch below, peering at him — Kuper.

His feathers were slicked down by rain and blood. Bare skin was exposed on the right side of his head. He squinted at Kyp and nodded to himself. "I didn't think death would find you as easily as that," he said.

Kyp struggled to free his wings, but his movements only served to entangle him further. "Quickly," he shouted over the rain, "there's no time! I heard Kym calling. Help me break these cords."

"Calm yourself," Kuper interrupted. "She's dead. They're all dead or dying. But I saw you through the crowd in the attack on the humans. And I'd already had the good fortune to summon your companion. So maybe that's what you heard." That's when Kyp grew aware of another, smaller presence, perched closer to the trunk. He groaned as Kryk stepped forward.

"Kryk," Kyp called, the inside of his beak suddenly dry, "what are *you* doing here?"

"I wasn't certain how to contact you," Kuper answered for him as he stalked to a spot directly beneath Kyp. "But if I sent for your Kryk, I thought there might be a chance he could persuade you to return." He glanced over at Kryk. "It was a very good imitation he did, don't you think?"

"He asked me to copy Kym," Kryk explained miserably. "He didn't tell me why." He glanced up at the dangling Kyp. "He didn't tell me who I was calling for. Sorry."

"When have you ever needed a reason?" Kuper interrupted, his voice turning hard. "I said I needed help. You've helped. Did you expect to receive food in return?"

"No, but," Kryk called over the wind, "what about my place in the flock?" Kuper didn't answer and Kryk stepped forward. "You said you'd find me a place. I have nowhere to go."

The wind jarred the tree, jerking Kyp back and forth and shaking the branch Kuper clung to. "What flock? The flock of the dead? The flock of the burnt, blasted, dismembered? Only *your* kind have survived — and me. Nowhere to go," Kuper repeated. "Maybe," he shouted suddenly, lifting his voice, "*that* is the Maker's message to us!" He glanced directly up at Kyp. "Nowhere to go, but away. Away from here. To the Maker's roost. If we can't have the life we were promised, we can at least embrace the death we choose."

"Kuper," Kyp said urgently, "help me down. Guide the rest of the survivors away. It's not too late to save who we can save."

Kuper snorted. "Late? It is *all* too late, Cousin. Too late, too soon and too hard to endure. All that remains is to decide whether we are to be swallowed by the human and digested or whether we lodge in its throat to choke it."

"Kuper —" Kryk plucked at the big bird's feathers.

"Don't touch me!" Kuper snapped, his feathers bristling. "Get away from here!"

Kryk quailed. "But I can't leave here without you. The others would come after me."

Kuper bent his head in close. "And what's that to me?" he hissed.

Kryk took another step closer. "*You* sent for me. *You* said you could fix things if I helped —"

"*You* were willing to do whatever you had to and didn't care what happened to anyone else."

"And *you* used him," Kyp shouted down, "just like humans used him!"

"Don't you," Kuper snarled, the featherless portion of his face flushing red, "compare me to *them*."

"You promised," Kryk repeated, "you promised that you'd find me a place."

"I did," Kuper replied. "And that place," he said, lifting his wings and throwing himself forward, "is *here*."

"Kuper!" Kyp shouted as the wind gusted and spun him around. A flailing branch clipped against Kyp's left side, halting his spinning. When he looked own, he saw Kryk lying still in the mud and runoff, Kuper looming over him.

Struggling not to be blown over in the howling wind, Kuper slowly turned from Kryk and looked up. His eyes locked with Kyp's. "And now to the end of things — of hope, the Urkana, the Collection," he said, raising his wings again, "and *you*." He flew at Kyp. It is the Maker's whim, however, that the things that trouble us most sometimes prove our greatest ally. The wind swatted Kyp sideways at the same time that Kuper lunged. Using his one chance, Kyp stretched his neck forward and grasped Kuper by his outstretched right leg. He tugged hard and flipped Kuper upside down.

There the two hung, buffeted by wind and drenched by rain.

Kyp's neck and jaw muscles strained as he firmly held on to the struggling bird. He knew that the moment he released Kuper, there would be nothing to prevent his death. He couldn't think of any other solution, so he clamped tight and hung on.

Kuper cursed, wrestled and clawed. He raked Kyp repeatedly, struck him with his forewings, dug his talons deep into Kyp's right shoulder and pushed. Kyp could feel the talons penetrate his flesh, slicing down past muscle to the bone. At last, unable to hold on any longer, he let go.

CHAPTER 40

"Now what?" Kyf whispered to me.

"We didn't come all this way just to be captured by humans again," Kym whispered.

Kymnyt stared with wide eyes at the humans, her tail flicking madly. "We're cursed," she muttered. "From the First Flight. Cursed."

"Quiet. It's only a curse," Erkala declared, curiously calm, "if we fail. Kym?"

"Yes?"

"You know humans better than anyone. Can you use that?" Erkala asked. "Can you see anything in here that would help?"

Kym tucked her head into her shoulders, a habit

I'd come to realize meant she was thinking. "Kata?" she asked me at last.

"What?" I whispered.

"When we were flying behind the moving boxes, do you remember?" She stopped mid-sentence, as though half recollecting something.

"Remember *what*?" Kymnyt asked.

Kyf glared at her. "Shh! Let her think."

"On the sides of the boxes," Kym said slowly. "Inside. I watched the humans, and I seem to remember there's a *thing* they do."

I waited, but she didn't offer me any more than that. "A *thing*?" I repeated.

"A thing they touch that opens other things."

"What things?" Kymnyt interrupted.

"Shh!" I hissed. "What do you mean?" I asked Kym, trying not to sound as frustrated or anxious as I felt.

"Back when I was in among the humans at their roost," she explained patiently, as though we had all the time in the world. "You used a hook sort of thing to open my weave. You pulled it up and that caused something else to spring open. I think it's the same here. Only the humans touch or press something with their paws."

I stared at her and thought back to when we had followed the boxes and I'd studied the humans. I seemed to remember them making a movement with their paws, and then … sticking their limbs out into the rushing air. "Yes," I said, recalling. "There *was* something! Something along the edges of the boxes that they pushed. Or rubbed." I stared at her. "Will it work if we peck at it?"

She nodded. "It might. If …"

"What is she talking about?" Kymnyt asked.

"Shh!" Kyf and Erkala hushed her at once. "If *what*?"

"If it works the same in this box, as it did in the others I saw," Kym answered. "It might not."

The moving box bounced, throwing us all into the air. "Where is the spot?" Erkala demanded.

"I'm not sure. I've only glanced at it from the outside. I'll need to search more closely. I'm pretty certain it's up there." Kym nodded her head toward the humans. "You'll have to keep their attention off me." She stepped around me. "I'll see what I can find. If they glance back, distract them." And she hopped off.

"*Distract* them?" I repeated to myself. "How?"

The human box shuddered, tilted, and we all slid to one side. Kym picked herself up and hopped resolutely toward the humans. We peeked from our hidden spot as she abruptly halted, then studied the walls of the human box.

"Anything?" Kyf hissed.

"Not yet," Kym replied softly. She leaned closer to the wall and tapped at it gently. Nothing happened. She craned her neck and tapped another portion.

Suddenly one of the humans craned its shaggy head about and glanced back.

"Kym?" Kyf called, her voice rising. "One of them has turned."

The human barked something, and the other turned.

"I think I nearly have a notion of what to do," Kym whispered urgently. "Now would be a good time to distract them."

There she was talking distraction again. "How?" I repeated.

"The Maker sent me across the ocean for a reason," Erkala said and opened her wings. She turned, looked me intently in the eye and whispered, "If I don't see you again, Good eating." Then she launched herself.

I stared wide-eyed as she sailed directly at the human.

"Maker of the Maker," I groaned and followed her.

There was no room to maneuver in the cramped, humid space of the human's box, no place for any tricks of flight. Wherever you turned there was human, and still more human. The struggle seemed to stretch forever, but couldn't have lasted more than moments. The humans, startled by our sudden appearance, howled and flailed. Erkala was everywhere at once — first on a human's shoulders, then atop a shaggy head. As one paw swept up to strike her, I landed on a quivering human belly and pecked. Suddenly I noticed that Kyf, groggy Kyrt and even Kymnyt were beside me, pecking and scratching. "Don't stay in one place!" Erkala shouted. "Move back and forth."

"Move back and forth, *where?*" I thought as I dodged one blow and found myself immediately ducking under another.

"What about the stingers?" Kyf cried as she clawed at the other human, which swatted at her in turn. "Shouldn't we watch for them?"

"They can't use them in close!" Erkala shouted as she launched herself off one of the human's shoulders, "They'd get stung themselves. That's why Kuper and his bunch weren't hit."

"It *has* me!" Kymnyt shrieked abruptly.

I turned and saw a meaty human paw wrap around poor Kymnyt, enclosing and crushing her. Nothing could be seen but her tousled head and the tip of her tail, twitching crazily. Erkala didn't hesitate, but went directly at the human's eyes. The human hollered, released Kymnyt and brought its other paw up hard and fast. It caught Erkala and flung her end-over-spinning-end back against the stony surface of the box.

I landed on the human's shoulder and, cursing, bit the base of its fleshy neck. It swatted, missed me and instead struck itself with a resounding thump.

"Is she still alive?" I hollered to Kyf, who had flown back to look at Erkala. Kyf didn't reply. "*Is* she?"

"I can't tell," Kyf called.

Then Erkala opened her eyes.

I flew past her. "Are you all right?" I shouted.

She nodded, and I curled back toward the humans. With Kyf, Erkala and Kym at the rear and only Kymnyt, Kyrt and me to concentrate on, the humans suddenly became much more focused. In desperation I slipped under one blow, perched on a human's nose and planted a peck directly between its eyes.

Suddenly, the moving box struck something. It jolted, shimmied and came to a crashing halt. I spun head over tail feathers through the air and slammed hard against the invisible stone. The human lurched forward and cracked its massive hairy head directly next to me.

All at once I felt fresh air sweeping past.

"I found it!" Kym called. The wind grew stronger as a flat portion of the box nearest Kym slid down and melted away, creating a gaping hole. "Out!" she cried. "Everyone out!"

Erkala slipped through the opening, followed quickly by Kym, Kyf, Kymnyt and Kyrt.

The immense human head slowly lifted, blinked and stared at me.

"And that," I hissed, thrusting my neck forward, "is for Erkala," and nipped the human on its ear.

"Kata!" Kym shouted, peering back through the opening at me.

"Coming!" I called, threw up my wings and flung myself backward.

CHAPTER **41**

Kuper dropped to the ground and quickly righted himself. As he struggled to regain his balance, however, it became clear that the leg Kyp had grasped was injured and wouldn't support his weight.

The wind howled, spinning Kyp around, dragging him through the twigs of adjoining branches, securing him even tighter.

Kuper unfurled his wings to fly and threw himself up — and was shocked to feel himself seized and dragged back to earth. He struggled to his talons, glanced about and saw Kryk rising. Though bleeding from a deep wound in his throat, he steadied himself. "You said I would have a place," he wheezed. "That's all I asked."

With a snarl of frustration, Kuper flew at him. Kryk slid out of the way and stood, teetering. Under any other circumstances, the fight could not have lasted long. But Kuper was injured, he'd lost the advantage of surprise, and Kryk, though hurt, was desperate. He fought with the last remaining energy he possessed. As the two grappled through the hail and mud, something in the tone of the wind changed and caught Kyp's attention. He glanced up. Disoriented as he was from his position upside down, he had trouble making sense of what he saw.

Farther up the valley, the clouds billowed and coiled in a thick, sticky mass. As the sky swirled, a tiny dimple appeared in the center of the churning murk. Abruptly a thin tendril emerged from the clouds and rain and, like a tongue, delicately licked the air around it. Then it extended and, as if feeling its way, slowly descended. Grass-blade thin though it was, where it touched, the prairie erupted into a dark, broiling confusion of dirt and debris. That slender tongue trembled, seemed to hesitate and then all at once discarded all delicacy. In an instant it transformed into something tree-trunk thick and hard as a talon. And as it clawed the earth, the earth screamed.

It charged forward, casting aside everything in its path — trees, bushes, boulders. The noise it generated compelled one to listen and at the same time made it impossible to hear. With a jerk of his powerful neck muscles, Kuper finally dispatched Kryk, flinging him to the ground. Flinching from pain, he rose and stared at the oncoming coil of air, seemingly entranced. Then he turned and looked at Kyp.

Caught between conflicting desires of revenge and self-preservation, Kuper hesitated. That moment proved fatal. A branch sprang free from a nearby tree with a piercing snap and spun end over end through the air, web trailing behind it. It struck Kuper mid-body, and together branch, web and bird hurtled across the field, at last settling, wedged tightly in a thicket of willow saplings.

Kuper struggled to rise as he watched the writhing mass swiftly approach. Then a great billow of mud and debris erupted and obscured him as the funnel moved directly over top, drawing branch, web, willows and Crow into the churning vortex, leaving nothing but a gaping hole in the ground and the shredded white remains of roots erupting like bleached bones from the tawny body of the earth.

Kyp wrestled against the cords, flexed his wings, gnawed at the piece nearest his beak. The immense black form swayed closer, stretching from earth to sky. The outermost edge of the wind struck, lifting and then rattling the hailstones back up through the branches. Abruptly Kryk's limp and lifeless body was hoisted from the grass. His feathers shivering, he hovered in the air, twirling slowly at first but with increasing speed. His wings — loose at his side — rose and dipped eerily, as though bidding Kyp good-bye one last time, then he too was drawn into the dark, insatiable mouth.

At last the writhing spout struck Kyp's tree full on. The noise, already unthinkable, became unbearable, indescribable. Kyp could sense rather than see the upper branches snapping and felt a rain of twigs and debris striking him. Bound so tightly, he was unable to move even his neck anymore, Kyp could feel intense, violent tremors quiver through the trunk as it shuddered madly under the wind's crushing force. Several branches above him, the trunk groaned as though in pain. Then — wrenched in the same terrible, relentless twisting motion as the air around it — it abruptly exploded with a deafening crack into a thousand sharp-edged shards that were instantly swept up and consumed. Kyp was struck on the side of his head and heard no more.

CHAPTER 42

We searched the bruised landscape for Kyp for the better part of the next day. The dead were everywhere. We realized that he would certainly have joined us if he were able, so we focused our energy looking among the injured. Each time we saw a Crow limping through the wreckage, our hopes rose, and then were dashed.

Daylight faded, and along with it our hopes, when Kyf swooped low overhead and called, "This way!"

Erkala, Kym, Kyrt and I followed her and, after a brief flight up the valley, came upon a single, stark, mud-spattered tree trunk projecting up out of an immense drift of sticky clay and debris. Only two branches had survived the storm, one reaching up to the sky and ending in a jagged break, the other stretching back, its end planted in the dirt, giving the tree the odd appearance of a giant, dark bird trying to escape the ruins of the shattered landscape. Firmly fastened to that second, lower branch was a swath of web, and beneath that cocoon of web, leaves and accumulated filth emerged a Crow head, its glossy black beak barely visible.

We carefully pulled and clipped the cords with our beaks. At first we weren't sure that the Crow within was still alive, but we were encouraged when he began to wriggle, impatient for his release. Finally we tugged at one piece and the whole tangled knot gave way. A battered, bloodied Crow emerged from the shards and shreds of the web, stood, stretched his matted, mud-caked wings and shook them.

Kym stepped close. "Kyp?"

He blinked, tottered and stared oddly at her.

She steadied him with one wing and returned his stare. "Are you all right?"

Kyp blinked again before answering. "Yes," he croaked, "yes, I think so." He squinted through the light. "If you only knew where I've looked for you."

"And I, you," she replied softly. "And here we are."

"Here we are," Kyp allowed. "And let's make a pact not to get separated again."

Kym cocked her head. "I can live with that."

"Done," Kyp agreed. Then he turned and slowly surveyed the wreckage. "Where is everyone?"

"Most of our folk are perched in bushes down-river, resting," Erkala said. "The Urkana is scattered. The Collection? Same thing — though many of them are dead. Maybe most, considering how many were wounded. I haven't seen Kuper."

"He's dead," Kyp declared and coughed. "I saw it."

"Was it the humans?" I asked.

Kyp shook his head. "No, I'm not sure if even they could have handled Kuper. It was the wind that swallowed him finally." And he related the story of what had happened.

"No," Kym objected after hearing the story. "It wasn't the wind, and it wasn't the human. It was something started back before the Collection, maybe back before we knew him." She stared at the tree's cracked and shattered form. "In any case — finished at last."

"Well," Kyrt said bitterly, "at least the wind plucked up that mite-ridden Kryk."

"I feel sorry for him," Kyp murmured. "He didn't mean to betray me, and I wouldn't have survived without him. As lost as he was, he at least found a portion of himself in the end."

Kyp turned, stumbled and righted himself, and I saw him look about, trying to orient himself, but the landscape must have seemed almost unrecognizable. The river, clogged by fallen timber, had jumped its previous bed and swept aside whole portions of the cliff side. Immense slabs of sandstone had slid from the cliffs and lay in jumbled piles. Trees were knocked down, upended, stacked one on top of another. Debris, the bodies of Crows and the odd human object littered the surrounding area.

"What now?" Kym asked.

Kyp crouched to drink from the puddle at his talons. He gulped thirstily, then, quenched, he stood. "Well. We have permission to leave."

"What," I asked, "are you talking about?"

"Kwaku's prediction. It's all happened just as he said. Every part of it. The dead flew only a little after the rocks rose. So, as soon as we have everyone together, we should be done with this place."

Kym and I exchanged glances.

"Are you able to fly?" Kym inquired.

Kyp stretched his wings again, winced and then dropped them. "I'm not sure," he answered.

"Why?" Kym asked. "What's wrong?"

"Something happened during the storm," he replied slowly, "and I can't see."

And as I stood in front of him and realized that he was looking directly through me, I understood the reason for his unsteadiness. Kyp was blind.

CHAPTER 43

At first we were uncertain how to proceed, we were all so taken aback. But as Kyp was still able to distinguish light from shade and his wings were mostly undamaged, we developed an awkward system. With companions on either side of him, we slowly lifted into the air and called continuously to one another. Kyp, relying on the sound of our voices to maintain direction and balance, flew between us.

Most of our flock were already safely roosted up the canyon when the storm broke, so in the end we lost only ten to the humans. We gathered all our surviving Family and — nothing barring our way anymore — set out. News of Kyp's injury traveled quickly through the flock, and that first day of flight was difficult. Many had sustained injuries, so no one was inclined to fly especially quickly, but watching Kyp limp through the air — he who had been the most adept and agile flyer any of us had ever seen — was painful for everyone. He never asked for help. He flew quietly each day until his wings gave out, then would glide to the nearest tree. Perching presented special problems. A number of times he misjudged distance and fell, but he never complained. The flock took his perching as their signal to stop for the night and would often press close around him as darkness fell. At those times I saw how, the farther we progressed, the more the flock took special comfort from his presence, as though his continued survival somehow ensured our own. Of course, he never went hungry. There was no shortage of volunteers to bring back scavenge to his roost.

We traveled like this, at a groundling's speed, for many, many days — sometimes slower than groundlings. When we rested at night, we tried not to think what the future held for Kyp, unable as he was to fly on his own, or how he would endure the hardships of the following winter. Instead, Kyp and Kym huddled together and busied themselves sorting out which landmarks we should next anticipate. Together they set the course for the following day.

Three days after leaving the Collection, while we perched waiting for Kyp and Kym to arrive at a decision about how next to proceed, I asked Kyf how she had known it was Kyp fastened to that tree. After all, there'd been almost nothing of him exposed to view. She hesitated, then told me that following the storm she had been so exhausted that she'd briefly fallen asleep in the shelter of a rock ledge. While she slept, she dreamed of her brother.

"Kwaku appeared?" I asked, surprised.

"No," she said, "Kaf."

I blinked. "What did he say?"

She coughed and cleared her throat. "Things for a sister to hear, mostly," she answered. "He chastised me a little. Said it was silly to be mad at myself — or Kwaku. That neither of them was mad at me ... That sort of thing. Then he told me to keep my eyes open for a tree that looked like a Crow — and he disappeared. He never was much for conversation." She ducked her head and smoothed a wing feather into place. "As if I could stay angry at those two," she muttered. Then Kym signaled that she and Kyp had arrived at a decision, the flock lifted, and we continued our way north.

And it was in this clumsy fashion, from landmark to landmark, that we gradually made our halting way up along the spine of the plains and finally here — to our own Gathering Tree.

To here, Cousins. From the separate branches of our different backgrounds, from all the limbs and boughs of our collective story, we have come together through sickness, fire, bad weather and good, out of the confines of humans and the claws of owls. The Maker has, in her indulgence, even permitted me my smallest of vanities and allowed me to place the glitter I carried from so far away upon the topmost branch of our Gathering Tree.

It seems so long ago that I stole it from the human. Now it hangs and sways as a testament. Not to me or my struggles — I know I have only benefited from the wisdom and generosity of the Family that adopted me — but as a testament to the efforts of the many individuals who somehow drew together from every corner of the Maker's making. It's also a testament to those who struggled alongside us but ultimately were prevented from taking their rightful place on this perch. To our brothers and sisters, Kyl, Kympt, Keflew and quiet Kaf, lost to the talons of the owl; Kaleb, Kutu, Kyr, Kwyk, Kylwyt, Kur, Kymur and Kwaku, destroyed by fire; Kena, Kyfwu, Klatwyt, Korafu, Kelemnu, Kymu, Klaskwyt, Kwat, Korlu and Krytch, consumed by the anger of humans; and Kryk and Kuru, whose lives, perhaps most unfortunately, were ended by the malice of fellow Crows.

But this offering hangs above all, as a symbol of our thanks, because we have so much to be thankful for. That the majority of our flock survived the Plague and that lengthy, lethal journey is miracle enough. That the Plague appears to have only a minor effect on those it already touched once is a mercy and cause for celebration — or where would any of us find refuge now? But in the past days, it has also happily become evident that our Co-Chooser Kyp's eyesight has recovered, completely recovered, in his left eye. And if he can't see as well as he once did out of his right eye, if his vision of the world is diminished, his vision of *us* — his comrades and Family — remains uncannily sharp, his flight remains supremely elegant, and his ability to find a soft, safe perch at night remains completely unchallenged.

Now the time has come for many of us to make our way to the nearby nesting grounds, as Erkala and I will, as soon as we have concluded this particular Gathering and this particular Telling. But come summer's end, we and all our fledglings will gather once again to travel south.

Listen and let me draw this story of our flock to a close, as every story is brought to a close ... with the introduction of another story.

It is said that after Great Crow had fetched back the sun and lost Kaynu, his First Mate, a shadow was cast over him as though the sun had disappeared again. The Maker saw this and thought to herself, What is the use of fetching the sun again if everything about his spirit is made dark? The Maker decided to create another partner for Great Crow.

She realized how frail living things were, and because she was in a generous mood, she decided to allow Great Crow his choice. She created three new Crows and brought Great Crow to inspect them and select a mate. "I am wood," said the first one. "I am long-lasting. Claw cannot scar me. Hail cannot mar me."

Great Crow stalked away. "What good is that?" he muttered. "Wood rots. Worms bore into it, ants burrow through it, lightning blasts it, and eventually the wind pushes it over."

He hopped to the next Crow, who was a glossy, rich black and gleamed in the light. "I am rock," croaked this second one. "Rain runs off me. The wind blows over me. I cannot be eaten, cannot be stung, cannot be wounded. I do not feel pain."

Great Crow grunted, "What good is that? Rock wears and chips. Water scours it. Cold cracks it. Let me see this other one."

The third was the smallest of the three Crows, made from the same stuff that we are made of. "I am flesh and feathers," she said. "I bleed. I age. I die."

"Ah, that's the stuff," said Great Crow. "You feel. You struggle. You recover. And through the stories you tell and the spirit you share, you will outlive wood and rock and all the things of this Earth."

And together, frail and resilient, these two met the next day and all its troubles ... and created all of the future generations of Crows. Us. Us, my Cousins, us.

Night is falling. Stars are just beginning to settle quietly in the outstretched limbs of our Gathering Tree. See them — the shimmering souls of our ancestors looking down to us, bidding us well, lending strength, offering hope. They glance back through the evening mist to First Times and ahead to the farthest point of the future and wish us Fair flying, Safe roosting, and Good eating, my Cousins.

Brothers, sisters, roost well and dream deeply. We wake tomorrow to make our way to the nesting grounds, sure that the next generation will join us in our long flight, a flight that began before our great-grandparents hatched and will continue when we ourselves are only stories.

Good Eating, Cousins, today, tomorrow and all the tomorrows to follow.

ACKNOWLEDGMENTS

Many thanks to all those who were there from the beginning and have since watched the chicks fledge and take flight. The Martinis, Foggos and Lamoureuxs. The people at Kids Can who worked so diligently to make this book and this series everything it could be. Charis Wahl, my genial editor and fellow crow enthusiast. Janine Cheeseman. All the thoughtful, dedicated folk who read rough drafts and offered their helpful comments: the Mother/Daughter Book Club crew, the Baxters, Dykstras, Lunns, Poriskys, Strongs and Towers; Janet Lee-Evoy; Katie, Jason, Betty and John Poulsen; Emily, Anna and Brian Cooley and Mary Ann Wilson and Nathan Kopjar.

A Family Tree

The Six Great Clans of the Family Kinaar

The Maker creates Great Crow

•

Great Crow & Kaynu Firstmate
Build the first nest, lay the first brood,
which hatches to become the six male crows

Kwakayla & Kemu the Hero & Ur-Kata & Ur-Kapa &
Kran and Great Crow reborn

•

Great Crow & Ur-Kala Nextpair, the Maker's blessing
Lay the second brood,
which hatches to become the six female crows

Ur-Kyn & Ur-Kar & Kela & Kyn &
Kymkalyk & Kwa the Wise

•

From the matchings of these first two broods,
all crows of this world are descended

Kwakayla paired with Ur-Kar
Ur-Kata paired with Kela
Ur-Kapa paired with Kyn
Kran paired with Kymkalyk
Kemu the Hero paired with Ur-Kyn
Kwa the Wise paired with Kwylyt son of Ur-Kata and Kela

•

From the pairing of Kemu the Hero & Ur-Kyn down the
thousand generations to

Klara the Eldest, who paired with Kinaar Wind Rider
From this pairing were hatched

Kemna, Kelk, Koorda, Kurea, Kark and Kush,
namesakes of the six great Clans of the Family Kinaar

Feather and Bone:
The Crow Chronicles

Feather and Bone: The Crow Chronicles trilogy is told from
the point of view of the Kinaar, a proud family of crows with
longstanding customs and traditions. Written in the style of an
ancient saga, the story highlights their struggle to stay together.
Through the heroic efforts of a handful of chosen crows, the
flock weathers a period of internal strife, plague and war.

Book One: The Mob

The Kinaar meet every year at the ancient
Gathering Tree. This year begins as one of
the greatest Gatherings ever, until tragedy
strikes. A marauding cat kills a defenseless
newling named Klea, and the impulsive Kyp
retaliates by leading a revenge attack on the
feline. But the Kinaar Elder punishes Kyp

for thus endangering the flock. The judgment is controversial.
Then, an unexpected spring blizzard spells trouble for the
family and they must split up to find shelter. Some crows take
shelter underground, which crow law forbids. Others find
shelter in human roosts — also taboo to crows. During the
deadly struggle that follows, two young crows, Kyp and Kym,
show courage and daring as they lead the flock away from the
edge of doom.

Written by Clem Martini
HCJ ISBN-13: 978-1-55337-574-6
PB ISBN-13: 978-1-55337-664-4

Book Two: The Plague

After a mysterious plague strikes the crows'
homeland, Kym is captured by humans and
taken far to the east. Kyp, alone and ailing,
is nearly killed by a former Kinaar crow,
Kuper, who is jealous of Kyp and furious at
being left for dead during a battle with a
cat. Kyp makes a daring escape from the
vengeful Kuper and begins a long journey through desolate,
plague-ravaged lands in search of Kym. A crow without a flock
flies in dangerous skies, and Kyp has no one to keep watch or
provide warning when danger threatens. Gradually other crows
join in his quest deep into the heart of a vast colony, where
they must survive in close contact with the beings they fear
most — humans.

Written by Clem Martini
HCJ ISBN-13: 978-1-55337-666-8
PB ISBN-13: 978-1-55337-667-5